Kids Power Academy

SUPERNOVA PANDEMIC

■ Like & Follow

Art & Creative Director
Lady JJ

Executive Director
Cherry Bee

Consulting Editor
Mr. Timothy Forner

Lead Author & Editor

Alia Spring Kong, 10

Contributing author...**Ryder** Chow, 7
Contributing author...**Vicky Ding, 12**

Main Contributor...**Alina** Chao, 12
Main Contributor...**Catherine** Chao, 11
Main Contributor...**Joia Zhao,** 11

Illustrators

Alia Spring Kong, 10
Vicky Ding, 12

Artists

Jason Chan, 8
Ryder Chow, 7

.

"I would like to dedicate this book to kids who are bored at home, isolated from their friends and those who miss going outside during this hard time, and to health-care workers who make every moment count for those in need during this pandemic. I hope that this book will grant hope to those who are down and lighten a person's day through this tough time.

May this book bring you on a special journey and expand your imagination and creativity to many many universes."

Lightning waves,

LG, The Lightning Girl,

by Alia Spring Kong,
Lead Author
COVID-19 Pandemic Sept 2021

CONTENTS

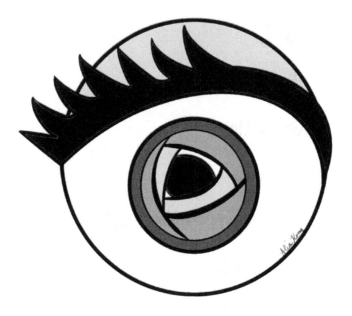

SPYS Star

Inspiration from...

"I was inspired by my Chinese school to create a planet called SPYS Star. The abbreviation of the school is the word 'SPYS' spelled backwards. Its emblem is the symbol of Ying and Yang, which looks like an eye to me. When the eye is halfway shut, half of the vision is darkened, while the other half is lightened.

SPYS Star contains a dark blue eyelid representing Ying, and an aqua blue eyeball representing Yang. The twilight blue center of the planet looks like an iris is the control room of SPYS Star Science Facility. It has many angled lenses, which allows the operator to monitor distant planets and stars from far away. The eyeballows are the defense system of the planet, disguised as the eyelashes. SPYS Star Science Facility is for all the top scientists from all over the universe. They work together to claim new discoveries and create new universes of Science."

■ Alia Kong, Lead Author
Sept 2021

1.

UNIVERSAL EMERGENCY

"Bweep! Bwoop!" A long… loud… siren alarmed the whole universe. A universal emergency message was sent out from Super Pathology Young Scientists (S.P.Y.S.) Committee of SPYS Star to all 100 billion planets and 400 billion stars in the dusty spiral shaped galaxy, the Milky Way. SPYS Star is known for its top-tier science research station of all the preeminent scientists in the galaxy.

Lady JJ was looking at the screen in the control room located at the main tower of Kids Power Academy. She is the most powerful superhero in the universe, but her absent-mindedness is very well known to all life forms. Her red sprouting fountain hair is her main signature. And she is the most respected Headmaster of the school universe.

Lady JJ was reading the announcement of the Universal Emergency issued by S.P.Y.S. Committee of SPYS Star:

"Attention all universal citizens, we are facing an extreme situation... About one third of our galaxy has reported an outbreak of an unknown virus. Watch for the following symptoms in infected citizens. First, many small dots appeared on the skin, and then crystal spikes flared up from the dots, and more and more parts of their body developed fibrous tissues and became crystallized. In the end, the host will be covered in crystal spikes. And they ended up suffocating to death. We recommend you doing the followings to avoid contracting the unknown virus:

1. Wear a mask or a hazmat suit before you come in contact with another life form.

2. Wash your limbs and tentacles before touching your face.
3. Stay in your personal bubble within 2-5 life forms.

S.P.Y.S. Committee will send medical troops to the infected stars and planets for further virus investigation. We will study and collect the virus samples for developing a vaccine. In the meantime, all universal citizens, please stay safe and avoid physical contact by all means.

Stay healthy and good luck.

Dr. Cherry BEE
Chairlady of S.P.Y.S. Committee
Director of Scientist of SPYS Star Science Research Facility"

2

Lady JJ was very concerned. Because the virus cannot be seen, Lady JJ does not know how much of the school is affected. She decides to evacuate everyone. Many students were starting to get symptoms. "This is not good! Not good at all!" Lady JJ was worried. She picked up the microphone to promulgate a school lockdown.

James from Proton, a technology wiz, invented a hazmat suit device activated by voice recognition. It is actually an innovative filter 'shield' which acts as a microorganism barrier wrapping the user inside, preventing any viruses or germs from being in contact. It is a one-way barrier, 'nothing' comes in but everything can go out. James integrated it into the Kids Power Academy badges, a yellow Star, that students wore to school every day. It is not very visible except barely showing the face grid as it is connected to the holocall and camera system. It is also equipped with a life

support system that can be synchronized with any space stations. James then was recruited by S.P.Y.S. Committee to work with SPYS Star Science Research Facility to produce hazmat suit devices and embedded them onto the SPYS Star badges, a blue eyeball pin.

3

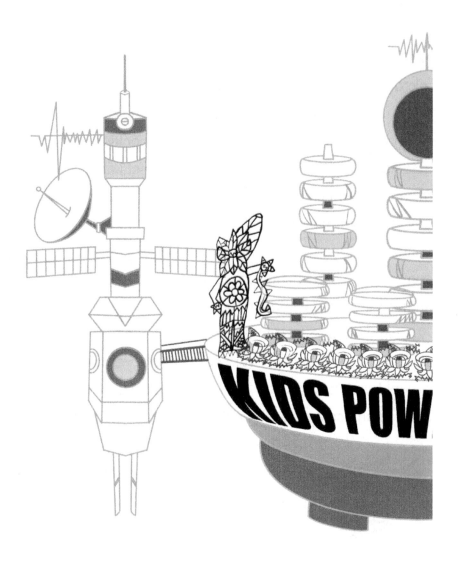

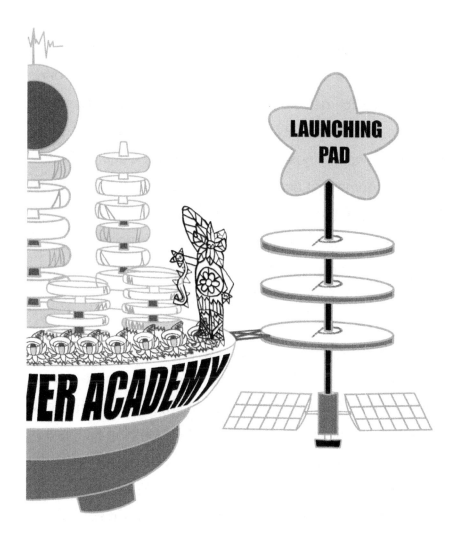

Even though Kids Power Academy was integrated with the most advanced technological system, it still could not detect the virus. The campus is situated in a space station near Sirius, also known as the Dog Star. It is 8.611 light years away from Earth and it has twice the mass compared to the sun. The star, Sirius, has a high range of luminosity which helps the Gurion Beasts to grow stronger. They are the bio-security system guarding the campus perimeter. The luminosity of Sirius helps the Gurion Beasts develop a dome that acts like a shield to protect the campus. They also have thorn whips to catch intruders. When the Academy is under attack, all the Gurion Beasts come together and transform into a gigantic monster. Kids Power Academy is the safest place with the Gurion Beasts on guard.

It had been a week since the school lockdown. Many kids were infected by the virus and were sent back to their home planets. The kids who were healthy also went home to assist the critical situation. LG, short for Lightning Girl, is a senior student at Kids Power Academy. She stayed behind to take care of the infected Gurion Beasts. They are technologically advanced plant-like creatures. Poison Fang found them at planet Guuwen, and planted them at the campus as bio-security systems. They are borealis green, like stained glass. They have red alarms in the center and

act like eyes to monitor the perimeter of the campus. The intruder will trigger the alarms, the Gurion Beast will screech. They look like salad bowls with cherry tomatoes. They use their brambles to whip the intruders and tie them up. Once the thorns of the brambles poke the intruders, they will be stunned and paralyzed. Those Gurion Beasts can assemble together to make a giant Gurion Warrior. LG studied them for the past year. She became the most intelligent student in all science subjects including Botany, Biology, Chemistry and Physics. She is doing a project of DNA re-engineering for the Gurion Beasts. She wants to reprogram them so that they could have reproduction ability. Currently, they have a short lifespan and cannot reproduce. LG's project came to a halt because they were infected by the unknown virus.

All of the Gurion Beasts turned purple and they felt fatigue. They were malfunctioning and could not stay alert all the time. LG found some crystal spikes on the Gurion Beasts sprouting from their petals. She had a theory that the crystal spikes have messed up their photosynthesis ability. It was releasing glucose instead of oxygen, and that affected their powers and abilities. The chlorophyll in the Gurion Beasts was also sabotaged by the virus. Their camouflage function was down.

Lady JJ activated her hazmat suit and flew in the air for a daily patrol around the space station. The school was already compromised with the virus. There were teeny tiny bubbles everywhere. The

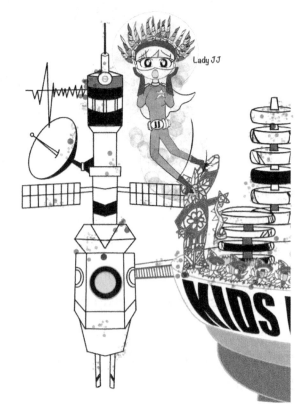

Lady JJ

close up of a bubble was a micro tiny pink dot in it. Lady JJ circled the space station and found a small amount of tiny bubbles on top of the space tower. She sighed. She holocalled Dr. Cherry BEE, the Chairlady of S.P.Y.S. Committee, her life-long ally and competitor.

Lady JJ said, "Bad news, our space station is no longer safe. The virus is spreading faster than we thought. There are tiny bubbles on the top of the space tower!"

"You need to leave the school now!" Dr. Cherry BEE replied.

"It is the Kids Power Academy, not just a school." replied Lady JJ.

"Yeah, yeah, whatever." Dr. Cherry BEE rolled her eyes.

"I need to check the I-CUP Café and the Wishing Tree before leaving. Please call LG back to the control room and wait for me," said Lady JJ.

A boy interrupted Dr. Cherry BEE and gave her some samples from Proton. Lady JJ waved to him, but he frowned. Dr. Cherry BEE noticed the frown and answered, "Ah! He is Luca, James's cousin. I will explain more when you arrive. I will call LG. Please wait for me at the control room and stay alert. Don't fall asleep again."

Lady JJ spotted a little girl on the screen behind Dr. Cherry BEE. The girl had a shiny crown on her head. Her cat was fiddling with a metal ball. Lady JJ was quite surprised. Before she could ask about the little girl, Dr. Cherry BEE ended the call.

Lady JJ went to the I-CUP café, which was once a secret laboratory and was run by James, LG, Dragon Boy and Pineking. Students used to hang out there and enjoyed special drinks and snacks that could restore and boost up their super powers. Now, it was abandoned. Lady JJ was thinking of the good moments and had a flashback.

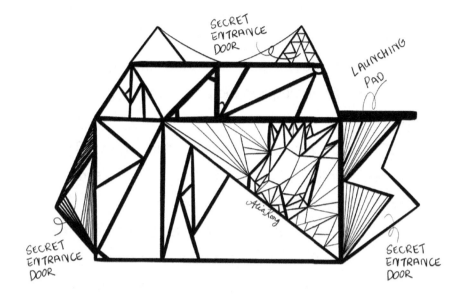

Two weeks ago…

Lady JJ, LG, James, Pineking and Supercat were discussing about weird bubbles appearing around the campus. Suddenly the Gurion Beasts ranged the alarm. Dragon Boy sent out an SOS signal. They heard a big scream from Dragon Boy, "Heeeeeelp!" The five of them rushed over to the ICUP café.   They were shocked! The whole café was flooded with Dragon Boy's poops, out to the door and blasting from the chimney. Everyone pinched their noses and put on their masks.

LG shouted, "Dragon Boy! Dragon Boy! What did you do this time?" She heard loud weeps in the poop pile.

Dragon Boy cried, "I can't get out by myself. I am buried in my own poop!"

Lady JJ sighed, "OMG!" She then flew high into the air. LG and Pineking dug into the poop wrestling with the sludge.

LG was disgusted, "Ewwwwww, this is gross! The poop is getting into my hair and my hands. It's so slimy! Bleeeeegh! Dragon Boy, show yourself now!"

Pineking said, "Oh come on... just pretend that you're the bad guys and those are the yummy cupcakes!"

LG was annoyed,"Are you kidding me!!" They wrestled in the 'Muuuuud' pie for two whole hours.

Meanwhile, "Ewwww..." Supercat glanced at them and sipped her tea from a fancy English tea cup.

Lady JJ joined the tea party that was prepared by Supercat in the air right above the I-CUP Café where they got a good view of the poop. She asked, "Aren't you guys going to join us?"

Dragon Boy was chomping down many Cheery Cookies, "Num Num, come on up and join our tea party!"

LG and Pineking heard Dragon Boy's voice and they were furiously shocked. They blasted to the sky and saw Dragon Boy enjoying the tea party.

Supercat exclaimed, "Eww...Blegh! Please get further away from us!

LG and Pineking raged like a boiling kettle and were about to strike Dragon Boy. James threw two Cheery Cookies into LG's and Pineking's mouths. They ate the cookies and calmed down.

James started, "Mmm, Cheery Cookies are very handy. They can lighten up anyone's mood even after being swarmed in a pile of poop. You two rushed into the poop while I opened a portal to pull Dragon Boy out." James took out an instant bath spray and sprayed both LG and Pineking. They are all refreshed again.

"Hmph, this is ridiculous!" mumbled LG and asked, "Dragon Boy, what was the emergency? Is this one of your pranks again?"

Dragon Boy replied, "What?! No!!" He explained to everyone that there were two weird men who broke into the I-CUP Café to steal the U-Power Candies. They were skeletal and tall with enormous heads and fat green lips. And they were dressed in black suits. They kept on making weird noises like Gu Gu Ga Ga. He told everyone that he was too scared and that he curled up and hid behind the cashier. He doesn't know what happened after that. Everyone sort of knew who they were.

Supercat spoke in confidence, "Again! How many times this week? Those Lipsies never learned. They will lose all their teeth one day. I bet there is nothing to do with their good old friend!"

Lady JJ explained, "The U-Power candies are very important to us. They can restore superpowers and boost up power levels. This I-CUP Café is actually a secret lab. LG was in charge of formulating new compounds to create snacks and drinks for the students. We need to find the U-Power potion."

James opened a portal to evacuate the poop into the Energy Collection Station near Proton. He brought out a feathery gizmo the size of a spaceship that looked like a duster. He used a device to move it up and down, sticking all the poop away. Then, he used his drone, Corini, to take the gizmo back to the Energy Collection Station. Proton was delighted to receive this energy supply.

Then, Lady JJ, James, LG, Pineking, Supercat and Dragon Boy swooped down to the secret lab. LG took out the U-Power potion from a secret compartment under the rug. It was a blue potion in a small vase with a chain on the cap. LG wore it around her neck. She informed everyone to activate a U-Power candy with a drop of U-power potion. She kept the potion in a secret safe all this time.

She asked everyone to remember the pass code, "Please remember I-C-U-P (I see you pee)!"

"No, no. Wait! I forgot! Say it again, please!" exclaimed Lady JJ. Everyone knew the problem of Lady JJ was that she could not remember more than three words at once.

Suddenly, they heard a huge explosion nearby. They fled to the Wishing Tree, a secret passage linked to Green Lips. It was their neighbor planet. They found a few pieces of U-Power candies around the tree. All of them jumped into the passage, like a long tube slide, and landed on Green Lips. There was a poop head, beady eyes with tentacles monster guarding the gate.

Dragon Boy screamed, "Poooop!"

The monster sounded the alarm to inform the King, LipsK, and the Queen, LipsQ, of Green Lips that their guests were here. Lady JJ and the team were always confused about this weird secret code between them. LipsK and LipsQ looked very weak. They invited Lady JJ and the team to their kingdom. All the civilians of Green Lips, Lipsies, looked unwell. Then Dragon Boy pointed at the two skinny men. LipsK anxiously explained to Lady JJ that his people were sick for a month. They have no choice but to take the U-Power candies. LipsQ described the symptoms that they

had, mostly they felt fatigue. They had no clue what had happened to them.

Lady JJ and her team had a good look at the whole kingdom and did not feel right. Lady JJ agreed to try using U-Power Candy to treat the Lipsies. LG activated the compounds of the U-Power Candy with a few drops of U-Power potion. The effect did not show immediately. Lady JJ told Lipsies to rest and they will revisit them in a week's time. Lady JJ and the team left.

During the week, students at the campus began to feel fatigue and there were tiny bubbles appearing around the campus. James gave Lady JJ un ringarde hazmat suit at that time, to check on Green Lips again. Things went south.

The whole kingdom was invaded by tiny bubbles and the Lipsies had red dots on their skin. Everything turned into a catastrophe. Lady JJ informed LipsK and LipsQ that she needed to seal the passage. She promised them that S.P.Y.S. Committee will come to the rescue.

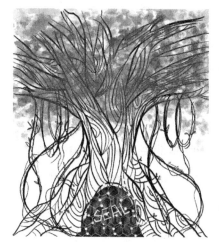

Lady JJ snapped out of consciousness and found herself back at the abandoned I-CUP cafe, once a secret lab. She checked the seal on the passage at the Wishing Tree and was still good.

Then she flew back to the control room waiting for Cherry BEE's call, but she fell asleep again.

LG woke up Lady JJ, "S.P.Y.S. Committee's emergency call!" Lady JJ answered the call and Dr. Cherry BEE appeared on the screen.

Dr. Cherry BEE asked, "I have been calling 45 times! Did you fall asleep again?"

"What? No! There were some technical issues.... yeah" Lady JJ lied. LG sighed.

Lady JJ continued, "Dr. Cherry BEE, the seal of the passage at the Wishing Tree is secured. Did you find anything that can contribute to the cure and vaccine development?"

Dr. Cherry BEE replied, "Luca is studying the Mitochondrial Deoxyribonucleic Acid (mDNA) and Messenger Ribonucleic acid (mRNA) of the virus. We had collected a few more virus samples from Proton, Planet M & N and Furball, they all have similar traits and pathogens. Tiny bubbles can be found everywhere. We are not certain if they are the same virus, we need to do further investigation on other planets and stars."

Lady JJ was worried, "It sounds like we need more time to find a solution! LG and I are ready for evacuation."

Dr. Cherry BEE called Luca to the SPYS Control Room. He then opened a portal to bring Lady JJ and LG to the Medical Center for disinfection and a thorough body check before entering SPYS Star Science Research Station. Dr. Cherry BEE welcomed Lady JJ and LG to the SPYS Control Room. Dr. Cherry BEE explained to them that James went back to help Proton. Luca was sent here because he has stronger knowledge in Medical Technology.

LG was the youngest Advisor of S.P.Y.S. Committee in Operation due to her broad knowledge in Science and her competency in resources management. She suggested a plan of dispatching four medical teams to Earth, Pinet, Green Lips and 'Unknown'. The medical teams will distribute the hazmat suit devices embedded in SPYS badges and provide two medical droids to assist the locals. Most importantly, they need to collect virus samples for the SPYS Research Team.

In the SPYS Control Room, Lady JJ saw the little girl with a crown on her head again. A cat was lounging beside her.

Lady JJ asked, "Dr. Cherry BEE, since when did you have the compassion to adopt amateur life form everywhere in the galaxy? Where did this little girl come from, and what's with this cat?"

Right before Dr.Cherry BEE could answer, the little girl approached them, "I am not a little girl! I am Dr. Crown! I am more intelligent and advanced in every subject than you could imagine, that's why I was invited before you." Lady JJ's jaw dropped.

Dr. Cherry BEE cleared her throat, "Please allow me to properly introduce Dr. Crown to you."

Lady JJ realized Dr. Crown was a very important scientist who led the SPYS Research Team for identifying the unknown virus and neutralizing it. Meanwhile, Dr. Cherry BEE called another young scientist to the SPYS Control Room. LG recognized her when she first entered, she was a good old friend of LipsK and LipsQ.

A-Girl   AIR Holocall   Dr. Crown

Dr. Cherry BEE said, "I believe you all knew each other. A-Girl was a former student of Kids Power Academy, then she left to expedite her science journey."

They were all very happy to see each other again. A-Girl told Lady JJ and LG that she was an Advisor of the SPYS Vaccine Development Department. Dr. Cherry BEE asked A-Girl to lead a medical team to Green Lips to collect virus samples.

Luca prepared four technologically enhanced MediPods for the medical teams. The MediPods were bright red, integrated with a 360 degree artificial intelligent screen and a 180 degree rotatable red cover that can be adjusted at any angle. The screen had an invisible force shield to prevent mild impacts.

The control system of the MediPod was connected to  the SPYS central control system. Dr Cherry Bee and Lady JJ could monitor the life signs of each team member once the hazmat suits were activated; and the camera would be live streamed back to the SPYS control system on the SPYS Star badges. The MediPod was armed with beamfires and sonic power for defense purposes. It had two medical assistance droids to assist in any surgical operation. The pod could also disinfect itself inside out and neutralize all kinds of viruses every second. The medical teams were completely safe and protected inside. Luca loaded millions of SPYS Star badges on each MediPod and did a final check of the systems. The four MediPods were ready to go.

Lady JJ then uploaded a photo of a dog, Monty, onto Amal, LG's artificial intelligence system, and asked LG to go with Team R to Earth and pass a small green box to Monty.

2.

EARTH

"Team R, assemble at the MediPod. Team R, assemble at the MediPod." Ms. D, short for Ms. Dominique, was calling for her team on the P.A.

Iris, a biologist, the Cat Lady and Snowball, a life scientist of SPYS Star, met at the entrance of the MediPod waiting for their leader to come onboard. It was their first time to go to Earth. They were excited to see its well-known beauty and the civilization of humans.

Cat Lady began a conversation with Snowball, "My home planet is Cat Star, like a rainbow cotton candy land. There are no other creatures around. We need to travel to our neighbour, Furball, for learning and training. I am very curious about Earth, although we are on a serious mission. What does your home planet look like, Snowball?"

Snowball sighed, "Ah... daadee daadee daadee..."

Cat Lady found Snowball a bit weird, "Oh well..."

Then they saw Dr. Cherry BEE, Lady JJ, LG and Ms D approaching them.

Dr. Cherry BEE welcomed Cat Lady to join Team R as she had recently joined SPYS Star facility. She was still getting used to the new environment and her new teammates. Dr. Cherry BEE told everyone that Cat Lady is a good friend of Supercat as they were 'neighbours' and went for the same training before.

Cat Lady interrupted, "I am sorry Dr. Cherry BEE for interrupting you, but I cannot understand a word of what you just said. I can only hear Ga gaaa gaaa."

Everyone was puzzled. Then LG went closer to Cat Lady and reached for her SPYS badge pinned on her blue dress.

LG touched the badge and commanded, "A.I., activate translator!"

Cat Lady suddenly overheard and understood many conversations surrounding her. LG showed Cat Lady the A.I. setting of her badge and how to adjust the translation parameter.

Cat Lady said, "Thank you! I can understand everyone's conversation now. I think the SPYS badge interfered with my hair pin system today."

Everyone smiled.

Ms. D stepped forward and introduced LG to Team R, "LG will be joining us to Earth. She is a local and has a lot of intelligence about this planet. She will leave to find Monty once we have arrived."

Lady JJ joined in, "I just uploaded the current pandemic report of Earth to your system. I think you should learn about local protocols before carrying out any investigation. Humans are highly educated life forms and very intelligent. LG can fill in the details."

Team R was concerned after hearing about the situation on Earth.

Dr. Cherry BEE encouraged the team, "All the scientists of SPYS Star are the best of the best in the universe. S.P.Y.S. committee put faith in each medical team of this mission. Godspeed, see you soon."

LG and Team R saluted to Dr. Cherry BEE and Lady JJ then took off.

Team R

Ms. D

Cat Lady

Snowball

Silver

After Team R settled down in the MediPod, Ms. D asked Sisi, the A.I. of the MediPod to give them a tour around the spacecraft.

Sisi sounded a few tones and replied, "Good day and welcome aboard. I am Sisi, the host and the A.I. of your MediPod. We will travel at warp speed and land on Earth in approximately five hours. This spacecraft is a sphere with a 360 degree full size screen integrated with a control system. The screen is adjustable in size as an opening.

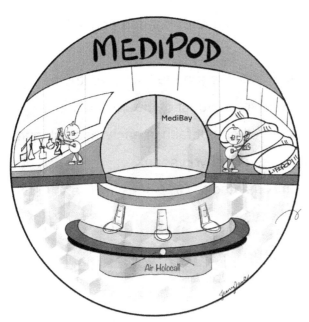

All information and holocalls will be projected as a hologram. It has a 180 degree rotatable exterior cover that can be adjusted to any angle and acts as a shield to avoid deadly impact. Inside the MediPod, there is a portable MediBay as a temporary medical station for the locals. There are two medical droids that come into assistance and a small laboratory with four lifepods. And if you need any intake, the MediPod has a full production line for food supplies. And I will maintain the essential supply of life support. Thank you for your attention, please don't hesitate to call for assistance."

Team R and LG walked to the two medical droids at the MediBay.

Snowball asked, "Sisi, can you tell us where those SPYS badges are stored away?"

Sisi replied quickly, "Hello Snowball, Droid M is the tall and thin droid who managed all the medical aids and equipment including the SPYS badges. Droid W is an A.I. surgeon and works in the laboratory equipped with a complete medical system for analyzing viruses."

After everyone returned to the main floor, LG asked Sisi to show them the report uploaded by Lady JJ. Sisi projected a glitchy hologram because of an interference in the signal.LG saw a dog and pondered, *"Who is this?".* It was jumping up and down and barking along the street. Humans wore face masks to avoid interactions, and many businesses were closed.

LG requested, "Sisi, please activate animal-language translator and augmented reality, and narrate to us the important information of the report."

Sisi rang, "I located three important messages in the report and will be streaming hologram segments soon. The dog's speech will be processed through a translator for everyone.

A website was shown with a background voice of the dog explaining to the team about an organization that humans had established for monitoring and managing the health of its own kind on Earth.

The dog's face was in the air and said "The WHO has over 8000 scientists and experts to take care of locals' public health. They coordinate the local's response to health emergencies, promote well-being and prevent diseases. The WHO had identified and named the virus COVID-19 recently. Infected humans would suffer from fevers, fatigue and dry coughs. The symptoms will lead to pneumonia causing the respiratory system to fail and most will die from fibrosis of the lungs. I am still observing the effect on domestic animals. We have no data about it yet."

The dog advised the team, "Please study WHO's website and understand the local protocol before your arrival. There are 14 days quarantine requirements recommended by the WHO for all visitors. And they must prove a negative report on COVID-19 test before dismissal. This is to eliminate all the channels for the virus to spread in the community. The WHO asked all humans to take precautions by following a set of hygiene regime. Humans react fast and create vaccines for healthy humans to prevent the infection by COVID-19. However the virus is competing with human's intelligence, it adapts and mutates before humans can neutralize it entirely. So face masks and physical distancing are highly suggested at this point."

The dog continued, "The WHO was investigating the mutated COVID-19 in India, called Delta variants. It transmits 100 times faster than the original COVID-19. I suspected that this mutated COVID-19 is the same virus as the universe is suffering from right now. I suggest you do the virus investigation in India and help the locals there. India does not require quarantine procedures. Please don't feel surprised when you arrive there. It is an extremely high density country. Some parts of it are unspeakably chaotic. They definitely need your assistance and medical equipment, especially hazmat suits. Good luck on your mission!" Sisi ended the hologram streams.

Ms. D asked Sisi to show the team about the environment on Earth and its current healthcare facilities. Sisi projected a hologram of Earth in the air, and started to narrate along with the images, "Earth consists of 70% water and 30% green land, and gives the planet dominant colors of blue and green. It has about 7.9 billion humans living there.

Its profound nature includes jungles, mountains, waterfalls and oceans; they are the habitats for wildlife and marine creatures. Humans continue to progress in civilization. They moved out from nature to live in buildings, communities and their own countries. Their intelligence even led them to reach the universe and established their own space station."

LG felt homesick and shared her story, "I missed my home planet. I used to play with Dragon Boy in the park and tame my lasso there. I love the conveniences of everything in the city. I enjoy the greenery trees and cool blue beaches with friends. Its nature is like a paradise. However, human civilization also brings many problems to nature like global warming leads to greenhouse effect, deforestation leads to animal extinction and drought, pollution can lead to all kinds

of diseases and viruses and more. The recent pandemic of COVID-19 not only cost humans' health, but also the global economy. Sisi, can you please show us the current situation of India?"

Sisi replied, "Certainly, LG!" Sisi projected a hologram of India on a world map and listed out some important facts about the country. India is the second most populated country on Earth. Citizens of India are called Indians and their official languages are Hindi and English. Indians took up around a fifth of the planet's population, equalling approximately 1.35 billion humans as of 2021, more than 60% of Indians are living in poverty, making less than $2 per day. The whole area of India is around 3.29M km². "India is a developing nation and the world's most congested place.

The environment may not be as pleasant as nature on Earth. There may be images that you may find distributing."

Sisi projected a horrific hologram of COVID-19 hitting hard on India recently. Indians were infected by the mutated COVID-19 called Delta variants, and most of them were left unattended on the street. The environment was filthy and dreadful. It was extremely polluted in Mumbai and New Delhi. Water sources were contaminated with amoeba. All Inidans wore face masks and looked extremely weak and fatigued. Their hospitals and medical facilities were overflooded with patients. Portable medical stations and COVID-19 testing booths were set up everywhere. The number of COVID-19 cases were surging, and there was no cure yet. Fatality rate had reached half a million. The WHO has approved a few vaccines that are safe to use which can lower the risk of having serious symptoms caused by the virus. However, the vaccinated rate cannot compete with the transmission rate of the virus. The conditions in India were much worse than they thought. It was heavy to see all those heart- breaking scenes. Ms D instructed Sisi to take them to India. They would assist the locals and collect the mutated virus samples. Everyone agreed.

An hour later, Sisi made an announcement informing everyone that they would arrive in India in 30 minutes. Sisi lifted the exterior cover of MediPod, a full size 180 degree screen was exposed to the outer space.

LG pointed at Earth from the screen, "It is so beautiful looking at it from far away! I miss my home. Hope I can revisit some of the places!"

Cat Lady added, "Wow! Earth is really a jewel. The blue and green colors are so soothing."

LG nodded and said to Team R, "You should all disguise as humans before you interact with them in India. Humans are very intelligent, but they are also very skeptical and can be very negative sometimes, especially in this trying time of the COVID-19 pandemic. They may take your help in the wrong way and might think that you are invaders. You should blend in and not reveal yourself as aliens."

Team R exchanged looks and agreed with LG. They commanded the badge to activate the shape-shifting function and turn themselves into human forms. Dr. Cherry BEE and Lady JJ holocalled Team R and LG to confirm that all their life support systems were well connected to the SPYS Control Room,

They landed quietly in New Delhi airport on Earth in summer 2021. Their MediPod was disguised as one of the medical supply aircrafts in humans' eyes. Team R activated their hazmat suits and got off the 'plane' with LG and Droid M. They all dressed as healthcare workers and were exempted for the 14 days quarantine. The airport was rather empty with no commercial planes on the runway.

Outside the airport, there were many COVID-19 testing booths and portable medical stations along the road. The government of India put up a curfew to restrict people to go outside and have any social contact. The setting of New Delhi was very depressing.

Ms. D asked Droid M to transform into a ground

COVID-19 pandemic
2021 Earth

vehicle to take them to the main medical facility in town. LG parted with Team R and went on to her mission to find Monty.

Droid M informed Team R that they were heading downtown to the Indian Capital Medical Center. On the way, they saw infected subjects packing the streets, many of them were left unattended. Piles of corpses were waiting to be moved to the morgue.

The signs along the road caught Snowball's attention and she said, "We shall wear masks although our hazmat suits are activated. Humans put up those signs everywhere saying, 'Masks are required. Please stay home.' We need to cover our faces to follow local's guidelines."

Cat Lady spoke, "Where? I did not see any signs?"

Ms. D told Cat Lady to activate her glasses for her poor eye-sight.

Cat Lady touched her hairpin, "I did not know my glasses had gone offline all this time. No wonder, I could not see any signs around. Thanks for that, Ms. D. Yes, I think we should put on face masks to blend in with the human community."

Droid M gave Team R a few face masks for their personal use and prepared a huge amount of face masks for the locals. They arrived at the main entrance of the Indian Capital Medical Center and unloaded all the medical supplies. Thousands of infected patients were rejected to go into the building and were treated outside. Multiple piles of dead bodies were scattered everywhere. Humans were crying and sobbing, the place was chaotic.

A doctor stopped them from behind when they entered the building, they thought their identities were exposed. Ms. D turned around and before she could explain, the doctor interrupted again.

He said, "Please hurry to attend to the patients. Cough cough... hack hack."

The doctor was dressed in a stained and dirty hazmat suit covering from head to toe walking toward them. He was in very bad shape and seemed very shattered, coughing along the way. He rushed to reach Team R and lost his balance then fell into Ms. D's arms.

Snowball spotted the doctor's name on his lab coat, "His name is Dr. Taj!"

Ms. D spoke, "Dr. Taj! Dr. Taj! Can you hear me? M, please do the scan and report to us!" Dr. Taj fainted. Ms. D continued, "We have to speak to their top authority about our motive and we shall set up a MediBay to help the locals."

Droid M reported, "Dr. Taj is infected and suffering from serious symptoms. He is having shortness of breath, and soon enough he will need a ventilator to help him breathe. His health is critical and may not be able to recover.

We do not have any cure to neutralize the mutated COVID-19 yet. We can only treat his symptoms."

Suddenly, they realized that they were surrounded by infected subjects; no exemption for healthcare workers. Ms. D instructed Droid M to stabilize Dr. Taj's condition while Team R assisted other healthcare workers and distributed face masks. Their medical facility had fallen apart. Many healthcare workers had overworked for long hours and were knocked out from tiredness. Just then, a man with glasses in a brown suit barged to the main floor carrying a heavy briefcase and holding many files in hands.

A nurse called out and approached him, "Dr. Hakim! Dr. Hakim!" He did not seem to hear her.

Ms. D stopped him midway, "Excuse me! The nurse is crying for you."

Dr. Hakim only wore a face mask and his hair was a mess. He had big eye-bags, and it seemed like he had not been resting for a long time. "I am sorry! I didn't mean to neglect any of these. I had to run tests on these compounds to get some answers. India has the worst COVID-19 infection rate in the world. And who are you people? Why are you in my medical center?"

Ms. D asked Cat Lady to attend the urgent matter with the nurse. Then she turned back to the doctor and said, "I am Ms. D. We are Team R, the top scientist of SPYS Star. I know you may not have heard of us, but we are here to help. Shall we have a private conversation with your team? I do not want to cause more panic."

Dr. Hakim looked at Ms. D with his eyes wide open and said, "I know SPYS Star! I heard about you! A young man came to me 10 years ago and bought all the green energy drinks on Earth. He asked me to lend him money to buy all the green energy drinks from the vending machine, over there! He said he needed to consume all of them. I thought he was joking and told him to contact the drink company. He appreciated me, as I was the only one who offered help to him. He told me that he was a  scientist from SPYS Star, and he gave me these pair of smart glasses as a thank-you gift. They are alien technology, and I kept this secret. The next morning, I watched the news reporting that all the green energy drinks in the world had vanished overnight! And our young future teller, Wina and her wolf, also disappeared that night."

Snowball reported to the SPYS Star Control Room, "Calling Dr. Cherry BEE, did you see all these? Who from SPYS Star came to Earth before?"

Dr. Cherry BEE asked SPYS, A.I. of the Central System, to search on the database. She instructed Team R, "Find out more about the energy drink and bring along samples back to SPYS Star. We are busy helping PineKing on Pinet, they have a more serious problem. Please finish the mission and return to the base without further delay. We will send you information when we have the results. Godspeed!" Ms. D explained to Dr. Hakim that they did not have any information about that young man yet, but they should act quickly for India.

Dr. Hakim led Team R to his office and his team was already waiting for the compounds to run experiments. The room was a complete mess. Tables were filled with old experimental kits. Papers were piled everywhere and empty energy drink bottles were scattered on the floor. Everyone wore broken PPE and gloves and seemed like they had not taken showers for months. Cat Lady used her microscopic eyes to scan the whole room and detected the mutated COVID-19 virus was everywhere. She found out that the virus looked like tiny bubbles with a red dot in it.

Ms. D shouted loudly, "STOP, everyone! I need a second, just hold still!"

Everyone paused in shock. Ms. D asked Snowball to use her pink soap bubbles to wrap up the virus in the room and she would use her biohazard collector to seal them. It will upload all the virus samples to the SPYS Central System instantly.

Before Dr. Hakim could do a proper introduction for Team R, a young man with a beard and glasses with a broken face mask dressed in black top and pants marched out angrily.

"What is this all about? Who are you people? Hack hack cough cough," he said, coughing seriously!

His hand reached out trying to slap Snowball's shoulder. Snowball dodged away in time. Everyone was irritated and expected some answers from Team R.

Ms. D spoke in Hindi loudly, "Calm down please! We are here to help. We know everyone is exhausted and afraid. Most of you already show symptoms of infection. We do not have any cure, but we will try to treat your symptoms for the time being. And you should follow the hygiene protocol recommended by the WHO. Stay away from any social contact and rest at home if you are sick. The virus is highly contagious. Do NOT touch anyone!"

Then Dr. Hakim spoke, "They are Team R, the scientists of SPYS Star. They came here to help us and investigate the virus."

The silence continued until Ms. D spoke up, "The whole universe is suffering from an unknown virus. The S.P.Y.S. Committee dispatched four medical teams to the nearby planets and stars for virus investigations. We hope to find a solution to save the universe. If the virus continues to spread, it may wipe out all the life forms of the galaxy."

Ms. D then approached the upset young man and saw his name tag on lab coat, then said, "You are Dr. Habiboo. I am afraid you are infected by the virus, M will stabilize your condition. Please follow M over there for treatment."

Droid M set up simple examination equipment at the corner and began to treat the infected subjects, including Dr. Taj. They did not seem surprised by the true identity of Team R. Dr. Taj might have shared his story about the young man from SPYS Star with his team. Droid M disinfected them one by one while Cat Lady and Snowball sealed the virus with the soap bubbles and put them in the biohazard collector. Ms. D used energy medicine, one of her superpowers, to cease the progress of the symptoms in each infected subject. She also prepared huge amounts of energy medicine pills for distribution.

Ms. D took out the SPYS badges and gave one to Dr. Taj, and said, "We need to return to SPYS Star soon. M will stay with you to assist your team. The badge is an advanced A.I. embedded with a hazmat suit device and a communication system. Here is the setting, you activate the hazmat suit by voice and dial here to communicate with us,

Team R. The hazmat suit will disinfect the user once it is activated. We only brought about a million of badges with us. Please distribute them to the ones who need it the most. We need to go back to report our duty now. We will return and hope we will bring along a cure to you soon."

Snowball took a few green energy drinks and asked Dr. Taj, " Do you mind if we bring these drinks with us? Our facility wants to know more about them."

Dr. Taj replied, "Sure, take whatever you need. Those energy drinks are mainly carbohydrates, sugar. We consume them when we are overtired and fatigued. Please come back to us quickly with a solution. We need your help."

Team R packed everything they needed and called Sisi to pick them up at the rooftop of Indian Capital Medical Center. Dr. Taj and his team farewelled to them and waited for their return.

3.

PINET

"Urgent! Pinet is in emergency lockdown mode!"
Pineking sent an SOS to S.P.Y.S. Committee, waiting for
further support. Everyone knows Pineking is the adopted son
of Dr. Cherry BEE, the chair lady of the S.P.Y.S committee.

Dr. Cherry BEE traveled to
Pinet to search for magic
juice at that time, and
found a crying baby in a
pinon farm.

She believed the
baby could rule the planet
one day. Pineking was
recruited by Lady JJ a few
years ago to attend Kids
Power Academy, a school
for superheroes in the
universe. His friends gave him a nickname called Pipleman.
Now the school was closed due to the virus outbreak.
Pineking went back to Pinet to help the Pinenions ASAP.

43

"I am the King of Pinet, and I need to take care of my people, Pinenions!" said PineKing. "I learned a new superpower in Kids Power Academy, healing potion and damaging potion. They should be able to save the Pinenions!" Pineking nodded his head.

Dr. Cherry BEE is originally from earth. She has telepathy and can control minds. She is a natural at discovering new science. Her work and knowledge had proven that she earned the title of the chair lady of the S.P.Y.S. committee. Although Dr. Cherry BEE is not Pineking's biological mother, she loves him from the bottom of her heart. And Pineking has great respect for his mom.

Pineking was on a holocall with Dr. Cherry BEE, "Mom, Did you see this? Pinet is in a critical situation. We are under attack by toxic rain, our pinons are rotting!"

Dr. Cherry BEE was worried sick, "Son, did you activate your hazmat suit? Do it now! Inform everyone to take shelters, and do not go out in the rain until our team comes to give you the SPYS Star badges embedded with the hazmat suits. Team Medic United is on their way. Stay strong!" Before Pineking could respond to Dr. Cherry BEE, she ended the call and dialed another holocall to Team Medic United.

"Hello, Dr. Cherry BEE!" Captain Smiling projected the call as a hologram for everyone.

"Team Medic United, what is your location? How much longer do you need to get to Pinet. Pineking and the Pinenion are suffering from toxic rain. They need assistance immediately!" Dr. Cherry BEE sent footage of the current situation of Pinet to them.

Everyone had a heavy heart after watching the video clip. Captain Smiling said, "According to Bobo, the A.I. of the MediPod, we traveled through a vortex at warp speed, and will be arriving in two hours."

Pineking's holocall interrupted. Dr. Cherry BEE put up a three-way conference call. Pineking spoke, "Our shelters were eroded by the toxic rain, all the Pinenions went to my castle to take shelter. I activated the hazmat suit on my KPS badge once I arrived at Pinet. So, I do not have any sign of infection. However, most of the Pinenions are sick and gradually showing symptoms. I am not sure what caused the infection. We need medical assistance right away. This is the coordinates of my castle, please come directly to us.

Captain Smiling replied, "Roger that! We will arrive shortly. Meanwhile, please separate the healthy Pinenions from the infected ones in separate rooms. We will bring along two medical droids to assist the situation. Please stay calm and hang in there."

Dr. Cherry BEE said, "Godspeed!" Then they ended the conference call.

Team Medic United

Captain Smiling is the leader of Team Medic United. She is a chemist from Planet Color. Also on the team there is Naky, a doctor with X-ray vision, and Little Porter with his dog Nono. They now serve the SPYS Star Science Facility. Their MediPod has a one-way system screen, inside can see things from outside, but nothing can be seen from outside. There is a table with buttons and control screens. The pod can camouflage and blend in with the surrounding environment as a protection. There is an intruder warning system. Once the intruder reaches the screen, the warning system will activate and extend the piston, closing an obsidian wall behind the intruders. Another sensor will detect the intruder and drop down walls to ensure the intruder cannot escape, even when the piston slides back. There is a button to lift the

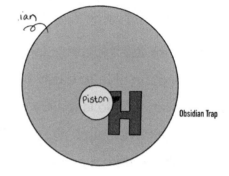

Obsidian Trap

obsidian wall to let the intruder get out of the MediPod. The entrance has a fingerprint scanner inside. There are two medical droids working at the MediBay. They look like small silver circles with arms that can retract. Their bodies have cameras that receive and analyze data. The droids conduct testing reports and perform simple surgeries. They can also repair the MediPod. Luca had loaded millions of SPYS Star badges on the Pod for the Pinenions.

Captain Smiling explained to the team that Pinet is near Earth, so Pinet has a similar environment as earth. Through the window, the team saw that Pinet's shape is like a "big Earth's pineapple", and it's floating next to Earth. Pinet can disguise and shrink itself to a regular pineapple, so other people would not be able to easily find out the location of Pinet. Pinet's landscape is mainly yellow, and the mountains are green with rivers and lakes similar to Earth. There are pinon farms that create a mask shape looking from far away. All the mountains are lined up into a short line. Overall, Pinet resembles an Earth's pineapple.

"THUD!"The MediPod landed on a platform next to Pinecastle. Team Medic United activated their hazmat suits when they stepped out of MediPod.

"Dooo, dooo, doo," the holocall rang, "Hello Team Medic United, I am glad that you arrived! I am working on my Pump drink to stabilize virus symptoms! Please follow the signs and come to my room ASAP, I will explain more."

Pineking, a man with a crown and a yellow shirt with potions timing belt in the center, was holocalling with Captain Smiling.

The pinecastle was a gigantic weird pineapple looking castle in golden color. There was a golden two meter tall pinon stone statue in front of the gate.

Then a soldier approached them; he said, "Greetings! My name is Justin. PINEAPPLE SUGAR HIGH!"

The statue moved backward and revealed a dark hidden staircase with bright light around. The staircase was made of stone. The team went up the staircase and entered the room. Pineking saw the Medics United team and immediately greeted them.

"Welcome to my secret lab! This throne room is actually a high tech chemical lab. My mom gave me the permission to build this lab so that I can analyze the virus in Pinet." said Pineking.

"I collect the toxic rain drop and analyze it. The rain is green because it is toxic rain that carries the virus Juice Bug. It is affecting all pinon farms across Pinet. Rotten pinons are piling up. It becomes a big garbage issue for Pinet." Pineking continued, "Also, our Pinenions got infected by the toxic rain. Male Pinenions lose their spikes and freeze to death; female Pinenions lose their appetite and starve to death; and

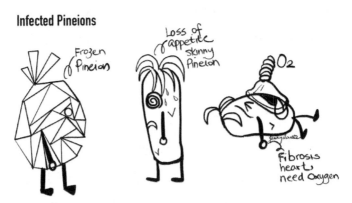

pinemals get very tired. The worst symptom is that it causes a fibrous heart. This means that their heart will crystallize, then the blood will crystallize as well. The heart will stop working as a result."

The pinons are pineapples on Pinet. The spikes of a healthy pinon are green and the body is yellow. Their juice can be used to recharge Pinenions' daily energy for a maximum of 10 hours. It is an important healing juice for the whole universe. However, a rotten pinon is brown with a stinky smell. Rotten pine juice is no longer useful in powering the Pinenions.

Pinenions are as small as one meter with peach skin and green hair. They speak their own pinet language called

Pikaboo. Pinenions have families and kids, and they like to live together as a big group. Pinet is actually still under development, so there are not many buildings. Most of the buildings are little shops and houses. They eat pinons and drink pine juice to recharge their daily energy. The healthy pine juice is yellow in color. It tastes juicy and smells fresh when it is in healthy condition.

"The toxic rain is corrosive and slowly melts through Pinenions' wooden buildings, so I came to Pinet two weeks ahead of you guys and built some non-corrosive shelters using special materials that I brought from SPYS Star for Pinenions to stay in. However, I am not finished yet and already running out of special materials. Can you please help to build more shelters for the Pinenions?" Pineking asked.

Captain Smiling heard about the emergency situation. She said, "Sure, we can. But first, let's settle down our two

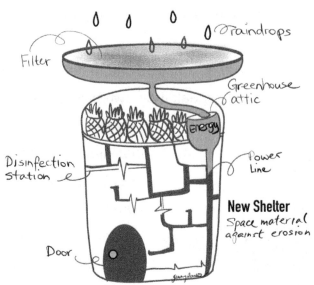

Labels on diagram:
raindrops
Filter
Greenhouse attic
Energy
Disinfection Station
Power Line
New Shelter Space material against erosion
Door

medical droids to help your people. And we bring along millions of SPYS Star badges which were embedded with hazmat suits and a translator that can translate to any universal language, the same operation as your KPS badge, Pineking. Now, we can understand each other well."

Pineking instructed Justin to take the SPYS Star badges from the medical droids and distribute them to each Pinenion. Little Porter and Naky assisted Justin to distribute the badges and teach them how to activate the hazmat suits.

Captain Smiling continued the conversation with Pineking, "I can help to build shelters, with your permission." She took out a magic, sparkling, pastel-colored book, and started drawing a big anti-corrosive bubble around Pinecastle in it. Voilà!"

Whatever she draws in the book becomes real. As soon as Captain Smiling finished, the pinecastle was protected completely with a dome bubble. Captain Smiling accepted the duty and said: "Your Majesty, your wish is our command."

Outside the castle, there are small Pinenion villages. The Pinenion villages have small shops and wooden houses that took the shape of a square. The village used to be filled with music and laughter, However, the village is very quiet now because everyone is sick. The team is heartbroken to see this when they enter the village. Captain Smiling immediately took out the pastel book, and drew some shelters with anti-corrosive bubbles for the rest of the Pinenions to stay. The Pinenions were amazed by Captain Smiling's magic.

Naky collected samples from infected Pinenions. She took a piece of spike from one of the Pinenions' body. This would be sent back to S.P.Y.S. committee to be studied by the scientists there. While Naky was collecting samples, she noticed an infected Pinenion was spraying a bottle of juice to his mouth, and he seemed to be getting better after getting the spray. It read "PUMP" on the label.

Naky holocalled Pineking immediately and asked "May I know what bottle this is?"

"Oh, I forgot to mention that I have created a special drink, called Pump Juice to slow down Pinenions' virus symptoms." Pineking continued, "Please get back to my castle and I will lead you guys to my Pinergy factory."

Pineking took them to the Pinergy factory, which is underneath Pinecastle, so it is not affected by the toxic rain. This factory is a Pine energy booster drink production plant, and the drink is called Pump Juice.

"WOW, there are so many professional Pinenions officers with hazmat suits working here." Naky was surprised.

The Pinergy factory consists of several departments. There are materials pre-screening department, production department, temperature control room, and research &

development lab, etc. it is a high tech factory with a lot of experienced knowledgeable officers.

"Two main ingredients of this Pump Juice are my healing potions and pine juice from pinons. It slows down the progress of virus symptoms and heart fibrosis," Pineking explained. "However, I am still working on the pump juice to see if I can advance the formula and stabilize the condition of the infected Pinenions. I hope to find a formula to freeze their symptoms."

"Sir, may I ask what's the proportion of these two ingredients?" Captain Smiling asked.

"I mixed three drops of my healing potion and 10 drops of pine juice together. The Pump Juice PH level needs to be exactly 3." Pineking shakes his head, "I tried to adjust the pump juice to different PH levels, but that didn't work."

Naky joined the conversation and asked, "What temperature did you set when producing this Pump Juice?"

"This juice is produced at normal room temperature but stored at -10 °C." Pineking answered.

Naky walked around and mumbled, "What happens if we store them at different temperatures? Will that affect the formula?"

Pineking said, "Oh, yeah! You might be right. Let me adjust the storing temperature and see if this can advance the formula of Pump Juice!"

Pineking was excited. He rushed to the R & D lab, and asked Captain Smiling and Naky to help as his assistants. However, Pineking tried to store the Pump Juice at different temperatures, such as from -50 to 50 celsius degrees, there was no significant change of the Pump Juice.

Meanwhile, Little Porter wore his rocket boots to fly out and collect the toxic rain in a tube. He returned and passed it back to Naky for prescreening analysis. Naky used her special X-ray eyes to scan the rain sample.

She was shocked, "Oh my, there are so many different sizes of green bubbles dancing happily. They look like oval evil monsters with red light eyes and four fangs."

Pineking wondered, "If we know what's the temperature of freezing these monsters, then we might know what's the best temperature to store the Pump Juice? I think there is a connection between them."

Captain Smiling used her pastel book to draw a spaceship with a shrink button. All of them got into the spaceship and pressed the shrink button. The spaceship became as small as the green monster bubbles.

"Let's fight!" Pineking summoned Dragoo out, and Dragoo used his ice breath power to freeze these green monsters. However, the frozen monsters were not fully killed, only paralyzed for a short period of time. It seemed the ice breath power of Dragoo was useful to freeze them for a while.

"Maybe we can ask Dragoo for help!" said Captain Smiling. Then they pressed the grow button of the spaceship and returned back to the lab.

They asked Dragoo to use ice breath power to freeze the Pump Juice inside the storage room.Three hours later, Pineking took a few bottles of the advanced Pump Juices out from the storage room and warmed them up to standard room temperature again. He went back to the throne room and used chemical equipment and supercomputers to analyze these advanced Pump Juices. It seemed that this procedure could further slow down the progress of virus symptoms.

Pineking said, "We need to run some tests on the infected Pinenions to find out more."

Team Medic United went to the Pinenion villages and distributed the advanced Pump Juice to the infected Pinenions. Again, once they intake the Pump Juice, it only stabilized their conditions and slowed down the progress of their symptoms.

"I don't get it. What the analysis shows us is that the new procedure can freeze the symptoms. But the juice does not have such effects in Pinenions?." Pineking was puzzled and returned to the lab to work on them.

"Woof, Woof, Woff," Nono smelled something and barked all of sudden.

"Yuck! What is that smell?" Little Porter asked. Nono kept barking at the rotten pinon farms.

"The disgusting smell is from the rotten pinons!" Pineking pointed at the piles of rotten pinons. However, Nono did not stop barking, and he ran around the rotten pinon farm.

"Nono has a very sensitive nose. He is telling me that he senses there are a lot of green bubbles around the rotten pinon farms. He suspects that these rotten pinons might be the root cause of toxic rain," Little Porter explained to the others.

"I asked my friend Bossypant *(please refer to Kids Power Academy: Superhero Assembly Ch.6)* to sweep the rotten pinons off into space. But the rotten pinons keep increasing because of the non-stop toxic rain," Pineking cried.

Team Medic United turned on a Holocall with Dr. Cherry BEE. They needed to ask for advice.

Dr. Cherry BEE gave orders to the Team, "Hi everyone, according to my observation through the livestreaming videos, there must be a linkage among the virus, toxic rain and piles of rotten pinons. Please collect these samples and send them back to the S.P.Y.S.

committee scientists for further analysis. They are useful information for developing a cure, hopefully a vaccine soon. And don't forget to bring several bottles of the new Pump Juice too. They could be the key to the solution."

"Yes, ma'am!" Captain Smiling collected all the necessary samples, such as toxic rain drops, advanced Pump Juice, spikes from infected Pinenions and rotten pinon. She gave the samples to the droids, and all of them needed to return back to SPYS Star as soon as possible.

Captain Smiling promised to Pineking, "We will be back with a cure. Stay safe for now. We will be in touch! Bye! Please wait for us!"

And they left. Pinet was a bright yellow pineapple with green pinon farms mask on, however, the color of the mask is no longer green...

Just then, Pineking received A-Girl's holocall, "Pineking, the Pump Juice does not work on the Lipsies! LipsK and LipsQ are infected, their lips are turning into stone." Pineking saw a horrible scene of Green Lips on the call.

4.
GREEN LIPS

Not long ago, LipsK and LipsQ from Green Lips had reported there was an unknown virus causing fatigue. Hence, Dr. Cherry BEE sent another science team, Team HOTS (Hope of The Stars) – A-Girl, Blob Man and Minako – to help the planet. A-Girl is a biology expert working at the Vaccine Research Department and is a potion maker. Minacko is a young scientist, assistant of A-Girl, and has animus powers which can enchant things. Blob Man has a scientific mind and is very helpful in identifying viruses. He causes trouble sometimes but always fixes them in the end.

Team HOTS

A- Girl

Minako

Blob Man

"Yes, Dr. Cherry BEE. We are ready to depart," A-Girl answered.

"A-Girl, don't forget to take some bottles of Pump Juice that Pineking sent to our science center a few days ago." Dr. Cherry BEE continued, "He told me that it slowed down the virus symptoms in Pinet, so it might be useful for Green Lips civilians as well."

A-Girl nodded her head and brought along plentiful bottles of Pump Juice and U-power potions. "Blob Man and Minacko, please remember to take good care of them. They're very important!" said A-Girl.

"Woohoo, I am excited to get into the newly designed MediPod!" Blob Man said as he ran to the S.P.Y.S launching room. "Let's board!"

A-Girl went into MediPod with the other teammates. HOTS brought along two droids with sphere heads and a cross in the middle and two antennas to receive and analyze information. They also have long bendy arms to carry medical equipment and help curing others. These two droids mainly provide medical assistance and help to fix electronic problems and complete missions.

"Zoooom..." The MediPod to Green Lips departed SPYS Star S.P.Y.S. Committee in a beam of lights. Green Lips is next to SYPS star, so it will take approximately two hours to get there. On the way to Green Lips, A-Girl told her teammates that she and LipsK and LipsQ are good friends.

She explained, "It was a long story. LipsK, LipsQ and Lipsies, the citizens of Green Lips, love candies. However, their teeth turn bad easily whenever they consume sugar, and it affects their health. Hence, Dr. Cherry BEE asked me to help and fix their dental issues using my special potion. And in the meantime, she also set a rule that: No Candies are allowed on Green Lips."

As the MediPod shuttled in space, a bright green planet slowly showed up in sight. The planet looked exactly like "Lips" with a slightly opened mouth where an energy liquid waterfall ran down it. The waterfall generates energy and powers up the whole planet. However, the team noticed some weird bubbles covering its surface and predicted they were the viruses on Green Lips.

"Let's find a place to land." Blob Man said and then pressed the auto landing button. Suddenly, "achoo!" Blob Man had an itchy nose and made a loud sneeze. The cup of seaweed juice dropped from his hand and spilled all over the control board.

"OMG! Why are you so clumsy?! Be more careful next time!" Minacko was angry.

Suddenly black smoke came out from the control board and "Beep, Beep, Beep" rang from the MediPod.

"Emergency Mode," the droid alarmed.

"Oh Nooooooo!" everyone screamed.

"Boom!" The MediPod crash landed somewhere on Green Lips, and everyone was shocked.

Thick smoke poured out from everywhere making it hard for the team to breathe. They fumbled in the dark Medipod and opened the screen. They activated their hazmat suits and ran out of the MediPod immediately in case the MediPod might explode. Luckily that did not happen. So A-Girl assigned the two droids to stay behind to fix the MediPod. Meanwhile, the HOTS team explored Green Lips. They all looked messed up and felt down.

"Only a few bottles of Pump Juice and U-power potions left. Others are broken due to the crash," said Minacko.

"Well, don't be sad. Let's find LipsK and LipsQ first. We have a more important mission to do," A- Girl cheered her up.

After the smoke faded, they realized that the MediPod crashed on a hillside near a flowing river.

"What are these blue bubbles?" Blob Man questioned.

They saw weird blue bubbles of all sizes floating around everywhere, covering the planet. The air was moist, and the whole planet was covered with a strong plastic smell.

Then they looked down and found out that they were on the edge of a cliff. In front of them were the floating kingdom of Green Lips, made up of land pieces which floated in thin air to create more space for the civilians on the planet. Each piece of land was connected with a ladder or staircase. However, the place they stood was too far from the palace, and they could barely see the tip of the palace tower. Minacko heard sounds of running water in the distance. Team HOTS walked to it and saw many unknown substances floating on the river.

They were about to take notes about it, but Blob Man broke in, "Hey guys, I think I found a secret tunnel."

Blob Man pointed to a narrow hole in a huge oak tree nearby. "Maybe it can lead us to the Kingdom of LipsK and LipsQ," he added.

Minacko took a further look inside the hole. She said, "There is nothing more in it but ivy and vines. How can we walk through this path?"

"I've got an idea." A-Girl took out a potion from her bag which had a label "Gate" on it. With a few drops of the potion, the vines disappeared, and the hole grew bigger and bigger, until the team could completely go through it. Dim lights lit inside the tree trunk.

"Can this be the passage that leads to the kingdom?" asked Minacko with excitement.

"Oh yes. LipsK and LipsQ showed me this through the entrance to their kingdom once. It holds up the whole transport system on Green Lips," A-Girl replied.

"Look! Is... is that... a... a... a... monster?!" Blob Man asked frightenedly. All of them looked up and there, at the very end of the tunnel, a poop-head monster with eight tentacles guarding a wooden door.

"Aaaahhh... Monster!!" screamed Minacko and Blob Man. Their bodies were shaking at the same time and they hid behind A-Girl. The monster looked exactly like the one Lady JJ and her crew met when they visited Green Lips through the portal at the Wishing Tree.

"Could this be the same tree at the I-CUP Cafe?" Blob Man asked. "A twin tree perhaps."

A-Girl answered, "Green Lips and SPYS Star were neighbors for many centuries so maybe they made this passage for special uses."

Their screams woke up the monster, and the door slowly opened. LipsK came out with a very sick look.

"My old friend, are you ok?" A-Girl said and ran towards LipsK and hugged him.

"LipsQ and I are very sick, and we have been in bed for a month. Some of my Lipsies right now are not only fatigued, their lips started to grow red dots, then the red dots will slowly turn into crystals, and it turns lips to stones. So here, we call the virus Stone Lips. The worst part is, the crystals will spread from the lip to the whole body, and in the

end it will turn Lipsies to crystal statues. I feel hopeless."
LipsK cried.

"Aren't the U-power candies useful?" A-Girl was
confused.

"Isn't candy not allowed on this planet?" Minacko
wondered.

"It is my idea." A-Girl explained, "LipsK asked me for
help one month ago, and at that time we didn't know what
happened. We only know they get fatigue suddenly, so I
suggested LipsK and LipsQ go to Kids Power I-Cup Cafe to
get U-Power Candies because these candies can recharge
superhero's energies."

"Yes, LipsQ and I secretly stole U-power candies from I-Cup Cafe through the passage of the wishing tree. However, the candy can only boost up our immune system and slow down the virus symptoms a little bit at the early stage."

LipsQ joined the conversation. She slowly walked to the crowd and replied in a weak voice, "The transmission rate of the Stone Lips virus is high. Almost three quarters of the Lipsies were affected by the virus bubbles in the air. The situation is out of control." LipsQ sighed.

Team HOTS felt sympathy for LipsK and LipsQ and promised they would do their best to help Green Lips.

A-Girl immediately holocalled Luca, "Planet Green Lips is in emergency. Can you please deliver the hazmat suit devices here as soon as possible? Lipsies need them urgently to slow down the transmission speed of the virus."

Luca used a portal to deliver the hazmat suit devices in no time. Then A-Girl's pet Cottonbell rode on her motorbike to get out of the kingdom and distribute hazmat devices to Lipsies around the planet. LipsK and LipsQ activated their hazmat suits and went out of the kingdom with the HOTS team to check out the civilians together.

They went to a village nearby and noticed that the majority of the infected Lipsies had red dots on their skin, and they lost appetite because of their crystal stone lips.

They could not eat and kept spitting green bubbles from their mouths. It looked like the transmission speed of the virus was getting faster than before. The hazmat suit could not help much, as three quarters of the Lipsies had already got infected.

"Doo, doo, doo, doo....." a holocall ringing from Dr. Cherry BEE came in, and A-Girl turned on the hologram projector to project the holocall.

"Greetings, I suspected that the infected Lipsies who had stone lips with crystal spikes busted out from their lips are the big carriers of the virus! The bubbles are covering the entire planet! I declare that Green Lips is in a state of emergency. Please collect virus samples and send them back to the SPYS committee for analysis!" Dr. Cherry BEE demanded.

"Yes, Dr. Cherry BEE. We will take action! However, please ask Luca to open a portal and send us back to the SPYS committee with the samples ASAP. Our MediPod crashed on Green Lips and the engine is not working," A-Girl replied.

"Sounds good!" replied Dr. Cherry BEE, then she ended the call.

Then Minacko suggested, "I think we'd better centralize all infected Lipsies in one place to proceed with medical treatments and collect virus samples. It is good to minimize their transmission of the bubbles as well."

"Sounds Great! Let's build an Epic Shelter for infected Lipsies then," Blob Man said.

Everyone cheered up a bit.

"A-Girl, do you still have your 3D crayon with you?" Minacko asked.

A-Girl checked her bag. "Yes, I still got plenty of them," she answered.

A-Girl first drew a big rectangle the same size as a football field using the 3D crayon right next to the kingdom. Then she drew the walls and windows deriving from the rectangular ground of the Epic Shelter. Every place where the tip of the crayon touched would magically turn into three-dimensional objects, and soon the outline of the Epic Shelter was built. Next, Minacko summoned some wood and some magic powders. Quicky, the wind around them started to blow; leaves and branches were swirling in the wind. When it stopped, a brand-new Epic Shelter in the color of jade green appeared.

"Cool." LipsK was surprised.

A-Girl assigned Blob Man and Minacko to gather all infected Lipsies to the Epic Shelter.

"Oh, I almost forgot the Pump Juice!" A-Girl took one bottle out and sprayed it directly onto one of the infected

Lipsies's lips. She was hoping for the magic to work. But after an hour, there were no changes on the infected Lipsies. The Pump Juice was not effective to cure stone lip virus. A-Girl holocalled Pineking and Dr. Cherry BEE immediately about this news.

Pineking rubbed his chin and said, "Maybe the Pump Juice that A-Girl had is the first generation, so it is not useful for infected Lipsies." He promised A-Girl and Dr. Cherry BEE that he would continue to do research and develop an advanced Pump Juice to help Lipsies and Pinenions.

After the holocall, Team HOTS started to collect virus samples, such as the crystal spikes from infected Lipsies's mouth, and asked infected Lipsies to blow bubbles into sample tubes. After finishing collecting samples, they rushed back to the abandoned field where they had crashed their MediPod. They need to check the repair status of the MediPod. When they arrived, two medical droids reported that the MediPod was busted and the engines were all down. The team was shocked and speechless. They were silent for a moment, until Minacko began twitching her nose.

"Ugh... Do you smell something weird?" Minacko asked, curious.

"Yeah, burning plastic smell, right?" Blob Man questioned.

A-Girl pointed to the area around their MediPod, "Look, there are so many green sticky slimes nearby. Gosh, it smells awful." A-Girl wanted to vomit. "Based on my experiences, I suspect there is a relationship between the sticky slime and the bubbles," A-Girl concluded.

Team HOTS took a closer look at the slime area and noticed that some blue bubbles turned into sticky slimes. However, why was there a weird smell? Everyone wondered.

"The smells get stronger when we get closer to the MediPod," A-Girl discovered.

She walked closer and examined the MediPod with her high-tech glasses. She exclaimed, "The slimes touched the MediPod and released toxic smells." She continued, "And since the MediPod crashed into the field and generated heat in this area, the slime was heated, then generated toxic gas. The toxic slimes produce energy for the virus. That's why there are more and more bubbles covering this planet!"

Minacko nodded, "Everything makes sense now. The weird bubbles are the virus and the toxic slimes are the energy to power the virus spreading."

Blob Man said, "We need to stop the toxic slimes generating energy for the virus."

"But how?" Minacko questioned.

Blob Man replied firmly, "We toss them to outer space."

"Are you serious, Blob Man? You won't just make pollution, but also cause big troubles by aggravating the pandemic to the whole galaxy!" said Minacko. She couldn't believe her ears.

"The slimes are toxic because they are on Green Lips, and only Green Lips. This is the only way to relieve the pandemic on this planet!" said Blob Man.

"You win then, Blob Man." A-Girl and Minacko agreed. They didn't have a choice. They needed to stop the virus from spreading continuously on Green Lips.

Blob Man used his superpower and turned into a giant bag to collect all toxic slimes. Then he immediately flew and tossed the slimes to outer space. After that, Team HOTS said goodbye to LipsK and LipsQ, and were ready to send back all samples to the SPYS scientists for vaccine development. A-Girl had prepared the two medical droids for medical assistance on Green Lips to attend the Lipsies and LipsK and LipsQ.

Blob Man said, "Okay! So we got our samples and we threw some slime into outer space. Let's get back to SPYS Star! I'm ready to – "

Before Blob Man could say another word, Luca opened a portal and said, "Everyone! Get inside the

MediPod, I will use a Toll Craft to bring you back to SPYS
Star"

Team HOTS were relieved to see Luca. However,
they peered over Luca's shoulder and witnessed a chaotic
scene, many scientists were running around like crazy.
Team HOTS pondered, "What is going on?!"

5.
UNKNOWN

In the beginning of the mission to Unknown, S.P.Y.S. Committee assigned IMT, a team of SPYS Star scientists, for virus investigation. Myria, a member of IMT, is the Majestic girl from a magical realm who uses illusions to make distractions. She is a Biologist and studies creatures with wings. Techer, her teammate, is a Robotic Engineer from an alternate universe. He can create medical droids and force shields. I-Boy, their buddy, is an Infectious Virus Specialist from Volth, a volcanic planet. He can become invisible.

Team IMT

IMT worked together for many years on the pathology of space microorganisms and viruses at SPYS Star Science Research Facility. They could understand each other very well even without using a translator. S.P.Y.S. Committee had tremendous faith in IMT because they have extensive knowledge on infectious diseases.

Team IMT assembled at the MediPod and did a final check-up of it before taking off.

"Guys, S.P.Y.S. Committee sent us a hologram," Techer called and projected the message in the air.

They were surrounded by images of the environment of Unknown. It was translucent and dull purple, formed by the shadows of all the planets and stars of the universe. It had no soil and no plants. The Unknown's civilians, the Knowers, were translucent as well. The facilities of the Unknown would disappear when it serves no purpose. It will reappear when the Knowers need it. This creates more space on the Unknown. The Knowers named the virus the 'Disaster'.

"I want to see the real Unknown. The planet is very interesting and mysterious. We will learn a lot about it," Myria was a bit excited.

Techer also added, "And I would like to take my virus detector smart goggles. I think they will be useful."

The IMT set the destination to Unknown and launched the MediPod. Techer put on a pair of green striped goggles and started searching.

He said, "It will take a few hours to go to Unknown."

I-Boy found something under his seat, "What is this? It has many pages inside. Is this what humans call a 'book'?" I-Boy flipped a few pages of *The Legend of Unknown?* He blew away the dust. "Why does it have dust? This doesn't make sense."

Myria inserted the book into the computer and generated a hologram. She said, "This thing is so miraculous. I've never seen it before…"

I-Boy took the book out when it was done and looked at it closely. Suddenly, it burst into flames.

"Ouch!" I-Boy shook off the heat and stared at the ashes.

"Don't worry about it for now, let's look at the hologram." Myria pressed the key and projected it in the air, everyone was surrounded by the images of a planet, then it narrated the story of the 'old' Unknown:

"The planet Unknown was called 'Unknown' because no one knew it ever existed. It had an evil leader named Evilzen who declared himself as god to the Knowers. Evilzen did not grant the Knowers access to other planets, so they could not speak to other life forms. Evilzen suddenly

disappeared one day, yet the Knowers still worshiped his statue.

Over time, the Knowers became blind and ignorant followers. Evilzen told the Knowers to offer themselves to the planet to keep its existence. The limbs of the healthy Knowers would gradually convert into Unknown's core energy and regrow again. The Knowers needed to sacrifice the sick innocents to keep themselves and the planet alive. This was Evilzen's evil plan all along. He planned to draw the Unknown's core energy and become a powerful 'god'. No Knowers noticed his evil plan. They and the planet became weaker and weaker. They could not protect themselves without Evilzen.

Until one day, a young sober Knower called Knowing revealed Evilzen's plan to the Knowers. He defeated Evilzen and stopped him from draining the core energy of Unknown. Knowing was crowned King and the Knowers followed him ever since. But they remained isolated from the universe with primitive knowledge. The only way to survive was by offering the planet their limbs as the energy source to the planet. The planet would defend itself from any intruders by cyclones and a black hole."

I-Boy, Techer and Myria gazed in shock as the hologram ended. Techer pondered, "Where did Evilzen go? He sort of vanished."

Myria was confused, "Maybe he put a curse on Unknown, causing the Disaster." As Techer and Myria babbled on and on, I-Boy zoned out and was silent the whole time.

"Good day everyone, we are near our destination: Unknown. The weather is windy and warm. There are cyclones every hour, everywhere. The cyclones are the defenders of the Unknown, it will neutralize any intruder without invitation. Please take shelter when you encounter them. We have 10 minutes before landing, please return to your seats and prepare for arrival. All the lavatories will be temporarily suspended. Just to remind everyone there is no solid ground on Unknown, so we might have a rough landing. This is droid Captain of MediPod. I hope you enjoyed the flight."

After the P.A. announcement, everybody returned to their seats. Techer tinkered on his force shield device, to prepare a shelter for the team during cyclones.

They looked out the window and saw a small purple musty planet.

"Are those Knowers floating in the air? They were like shadows, forming a big question mark on the planet! Are they asking who we are?" Myria questioned.

I-Boy replied, "Maybe... Let's send them a message that we are here to rescue."

Techer ordered the droid Captain to send an universal signal to the Knowers. The droid Captain flashed the one 'eyelash' on the MediPod telling them that they were the IMT, SPYS Star's scientists, sent from S.P.Y.S. Committee to the rescue. All the Knowers scattered around and formed an arrow to direct them to a landing zone.

Techer spotted a weird-looking Knower and said, "Look, I saw two shadows on that Knower, one is grey and the other is green. According to my smart goggles, the green shadow is formed by many viruses and they are manipulating that Knower. The viruses cannot attach to the Knower because they are translucent. So the virus mutated and adapted to the condition to control the host."

Everybody shuddered at the horrific descriptions by Techer.

The MediPod followed the direction from the Knowers and landed safely on Unknown. They brought along the

SPYS Star badges and a medical droid to treat the Knowers. The other medical droid stayed behind to monitor the team's life-support system and receive data from IMT during the mission. They checked in with S.P.Y.S. Committee on a holocall.

Dr. Cherry BEE informed the IMT, "Your life support system is stable and your cameras are on live. Godspeed!"

After the holocall ended, Myria cried, "We are good to go! Make sure you activate your hazmat suits!"

The droid Captain opened the screen and the IMT walked out onto Unknown.

"I'm worried about walking on Unknown? The ground is translucent like I am stepping on nothing." Techer was afraid.

I-Boy added, "And the ground keeps on flickering! There are only shadows. How can it support us?"

Myria walked carefully, "Relax. We need to adapt to this environment."

Techer and I-Boy closed their eyes and walked in faith, and it worked! Techer's robot, Bop, bounced around IMT and collected samples to analyze how the planet was formed. He communicated with them through his screens on his body.

IMT saw hundreds of Knowers scattered on the land. They were dormant, but still had a pulse. IMT can barely set a foot on an empty spot. They carefully move around them.

"Haiiyaa! I'm so sorry!" I-Boy cried.

They turned around and saw I-Boy stepping right through a Knower. The Knower did not react at all, it was not bothered by I-Boy. He hopped to another Knower, and then another, and then another, and then another...

Then I-Boy cried, "Hey, did you see that! We can just step through them. They are translucent and we cannot harm them at all!"

The rest of the IMT was unsure but they followed him.

Myria started, "Why aren't there any shelters here? And why are all the Knowers lying on the ground? There is supposed to be a facility, where is it?"

Myria told the medical droid to scan each Knower and check on their life condition. Then the droid shone a ray of light across a Knower's body.

The droid said, "This Knower has a green shadow manipulating the host. It is actually the virus. It infected the host with crystal spikes bursted out, internally damaging the body systems. This Knower is in a vegetative state, yet it is conscious. The crystal spikes adapted to the host's condition and became translucent too."

Techer exclaimed, "The virus is stronger than we thought, and its is very intelligent. It mutated to adapt to the host's condition. Glad that we have our hazmat suits on!"

"Look! Is that the facility of Unknown that was mentioned by S.P.Y.S. Committee? Let's find out." I-Boy suggested.

The IMT walked to the building and did not find any entrance. It had no windows, and it was one-storey. They saw many solar panels on the roof.

The IMT circled around the building and found a ginormous intercom system. Myria pressed the red button on the intercom. A loud buzz came from the speaker and a door appeared with a hologram greeting.

The hologram showed a tall man dressed in a lab coat with a pair of glasses and asked, "Hello there! I haven't seen any other life forms, except Knowers, for more than 10 years! Who are you? Why are you here?"

Just then, Dr. Cherry BEE holocalled Myria, "This man looks so familiar. He may be one of the long-gone scientists from SPYS Star! I will search up information and send it to you. For the time being, please pay extra precaution. There seems to be a magnetic force around the building that will cut off our signals." The holocall ended.

Myria started to introduce the IMT, "We are the scientists of SPYS Star. The S.P.Y.S. Committee asked us to investigate the virus on Unknown. We are here to help."

The man's eyes narrowed and spoke, "Humph... I once was a scientist of SPYS Star! I sent so many S.O.S signals to them, but they abandoned me here!"

Techer looked concerned, "SPYS Star would never abandon -" Techer was interrupted by a holocall.

Dr. Cherry BEE saw the man's furious expression and said, "Techer, can you project the holocall in the space please. I want to talk to Scientist 00123 face to face."

Techer projected the holocall out, Scientist 00123 immediately recognized Dr. Cherry BEE.

The man raged, "Why didn't you send anyone to me?!"

Dr. Cherry BEE replied in a low voice, "We did not give up on you. We have been searching for you all this time. We did not receive any of your S.O.S signals. I guess you may not realize your building was wrapped in an undetectable magnetic force. We are sorry we came to you late. Please join the IMT, we will take you home."

Scientist 00123 sobbed, "I can finally return home!"

Dr. Cherry BEE explained everything to IMT. Then she had Luca recode their transmission signal so that they could stay online as they entered the magnetic field. The holocall ended and the door opened. Right behind the door, was the real Scientist 00123. IMT followed him into the building.

"This is my experimental lab. I started this when my spacecraft crashed on Unknown. I was assigned with my trainer to Planet Testy for a secret project ten years ago. We met up with the rest of the team of SPYS Star there. I was ordered to fly to Earth to get some green matter then I met a girl and her wolf. They came along with me to Testy, however on the way we passed by Unknown and we were sucked in by the cyclone and crash-landed. Since then I lost contact with everyone outside Unknown." Scientist 00123 paused.

Then I-Boy broke the silence and gave a SPYS Star badge to him, "This is yours. You are a scientist of SPYS Star! The badge is very handy; it is embedded with the universe's most advanced hazmat suit device. Try it on!"

I-Boy helped Scientist 00123 set up the voice recognition on the badge and activated the hazmat suit for him. I-Boy also explained the device was connected to the central control system of SPYS Star.

Scientist 00123 was fascinated, "This is beyond imagination! I don't remember that we had this kind of technology when I left SPYS Star to Testy. Thank you. Let me take you to Wina, she is part of my experiment. When

Wina and I crash landed on Unknown, some of the green matter had entered Wina's body. Over the 10 years, I did many experiments on her to keep her life stable and she developed new powers."

The IMT and Scientist 00123 walked in a loooooooong hallway.

Myria was curious, "This hallway has no end!!"

Scientist 00123 smiled. "Yes, this is quite a long hallway. Sometimes I wish it was shorter," he sighed. "But safety is always first. The chemicals used on Wina are hyperactive and very unstable. The room has to be airtight."

I-Boy said, "Uhhhhhh... After we meet Wina, we need to collect the virus samples of the Knowers and send them back to S.P.Y.S. Committee for developing a cure, because the whole universe is suffering from this Supernova Pandemic, and many life forms are infected. Our medical droid can provide medical assistance to the Knowers."

Scientist 00123 replied, "Oh!! I have a collection of virus samples in my lab, but I am not able to collect the virus samples in the green shadow. They are translucent, no flesh or bones, unless you have a machine that can suck the whole green shadow in."

Techer nodded and had a blueprint in his head. The IMT finally reached a brown door. Scientist 00123 opened the door with a smart card.

The lights were rather dim. The IMT was shocked to see a girl sealed inside a big tank, connected with many pipes and tubes, filled with luminous fluid. Scientist 00123 explained that the luminous fluid is the green matter that kept Wina alive. She was combined with her wolf companion in the fluid. He checked his watch, "In two minutes, Wina will be awake and her energy charging will be completed. She can summon her spiritual wolf packs."

Suddenly, the room started to rattle. Test tubes and bottles bubbled rapidly and the lights flickered.

Myria was frightened, "What's going on!"

"Don't panic! I just need to lower the pressure of the tank and let Wina out." Scientist 00123 was busy turning the lever and pushing on many buttons.

Finally the whole room calmed down. The girl stormed out of the tank with a skeptical look toward IMT. She wanted to attack them, because they were strangers. She was about to raise her arms to strike, but Scientist 00123 yanked at her arm.

"Stop!" He said, "They are our friends and come to rescue us. We can finally go home!"

She stared at Scientist 00123 and swept his hand away. She was muted. She sniffed around IMT and then ran out the room.

Scientist 00123 felt embarrassed, "It is a bit awkward. Wina is not usually like this. Maybe she feels uneasy, because she has not seen anyone else for a long time. She usually goes for a run and will be back soon."

Everyone exchanged a look.

I-Boy broke the silence and asked, "Well, shall we go to your laboratory to collect samples and data while waiting for Wina?"

Everyone agreed and went to the lab.

Scientist 00123 and IMT arrived at the laboratory. It was a huge room with many monitors and many experimental settings. There were test tubes, beakers, vases, scales, measuring devices, samples, potions, and a few bunsen burners cooking some potions on the table. And on both sides of the room, there were beds with life support equipment. The medical droid started to explore the lab.

Myria spoke up, "Is this a medical facility for the Knowers? And it will disappear by itself when there are no more intakes? Why didn't you accept all the sick Knowers lying outside?"

Scientist 00123 explained, "This facility never disappears, Wina and I were here all these times. We treated millions of Knowers and helped them to regain their strength after Unknown sucked their energy to keep the planet vitality. However, this construction was covered by heavy smoke once Unknown turned on its defense system. I need to turn on the shield system of the facility to avoid those powerful cyclones. All the Knowners were infected by the virus. This facility is too small to accept them all. We are not prepared for such a massive need. I can only treat them outside."

IMT noticed that the information of Unknown given by S.P.Y.S. Committee had some parts missing. Before Scientist 00123 continued on, the medical droid, holding a vase filled with luminous green fluid, approached them and asked to take the green matter to SPYS Star.

Scientist 00123 thought for a while and said, "That green matter is very powerful. We do not understand it completely. However, I am using it to revive the Knowners and keep Wina alive. It does not help to kill the virus Disaster. I tried to use the green matter in many combinations but none of the attempts worked. Unknown depends on the energy fed by the Knowers, if they become weak, so will the planet! I need to keep the green matter for the Knowners. I can give you a few drops to take back to SPYS Star for further study." He then poured a few drops of the green matter into a test tube and sealed it.

He passed it to Techer and said, "I collected many virus samples in the last couple weeks. They keep on mutating. The latest mutation of the virus is that they adapt to Knowers' current condition and become a green shadow. And I am not able to get any samples out of it."

Techer stepped in proudly, "No worries! I already invented a super shadow sucker. I prepared it after you mentioned a sucking machine back in the hallway to Wina's room. We are all set to get more virus samples, now!"

Techer demonstrated on operating the machine, it blew everyone's minds, afterall he is a gizmo wiz.

While everyone's attention still on Techer's super shadow sucker, Scientist 00123 noticed Myria spotted a throne covered with blanket.

Scientist 00123 caught Myria's eye, "You have a question?"

Myria blurted loudly, "You are King Knowing! You put *The Legend of Unknown* on our MediPod!"

Scientist 00123 said, "Yes, I am King Knowing. I wore a disguise ten years ago to adapt to the environment of Unknown and live with the Knowers. I revealed the evil plan of Evilzen to the Knowers and exiled him to outer space. I help the Knowers to regain their health and strength. They are primitive life forms. They need to follow a 'god' image to survive. I explained so many times to them not to worship me, but they cannot understand. And now I cannot help them further with this Disaster. And about that book on your MediPod, I think maybe one of the Knowers went for space travel and left it in your pod." Scientist 00123 sobbed.

There was something stirring in Myria's head, but she could not figure it out yet.

Scientist 00123 suggested, "Shall we go out to collect the Disaster virus samples?"

Just then Wina came back and joined everyone. Once they opened the gate, they saw an endless field lying with hundreds of Knowers on the ground. Most of them were fading out and some of them were flickering more rapidly. The planet was shaking and also glitching. Techer used his super shadow sucker to suck up part of the green shadow and stored it into a tube with sealed cap. Everyone looked at the Disaster in the tube, the virus was more aggressive than its previous form. It multiplied exponentially and bursted out crystal in the tube. It was horrifying.

Dr Cherry BEE holocalled IMT to assemble at SPYS Star. S.P.Y.S. Committee needed all the teams to bring back the virus samples for finding a cure and developing a vaccine. IMT answered the call and discussed the situation with Dr. Cherry BEE. They decided that I-Boy would take the virus samples and data back to the station first. The rest of the team would stay behind to help Scientist 00123 treat the Knowers because they were dying. Dr Cherry Bee agreed, and the call ended.

The IMT gathered enough virus samples and returned to the MediPod. Scientist 00123 and Wina came along to help them unload their portable MediBay onto the planet. The two medical droids would set up a station next to the facility. Myria and Techer made sure they had all the medical equipment that they needed for treating Knowers, while I-Boy went to the bridge to start the engines.

Everything seemed fine until a loud, wicked laugh alerted everyone. All of them tried to figure out what was going on.

Scientist 00123 gritted his teeth, "Nobody is going anywhere on my watch! You will be fed to my planet, Unknown!"

Everybody took shelter and was shocked. Myria pointed at Scientist 00123, "He is the Evilzen! He put the *Legend of Unknown* on our ship!"

Evilzen laughed, "Mwa Ha Ha Ha Ha! You are right! I have magnificent powers! I can teleport anything and anywhere in the universe. I use the book as bait to take you here! I hate my brother; always in my way! He thought he could exile me and brand himself as King Knowing?! Hah! What a coward!" Suddenly, he grew humongous, as the size of a mountain. He banged his fists on the ground. "Now die!"

Techer activated the force shield just in time to keep everyone safe and helped the MediPod zoom off into space.

Inside the MediPod, I-Boy quickly sent a S.O.S. signal to SPYS Star, "Mayday! Mayday! We are under attack! We are under attack!" I-Boy realized his life support system was damaged. And the holocall system was jammed. He saw Dr. Cherry BEE on a static screen before it went offline. Everything was malfunctioning because of the big impact.

Techer's force field got tossed away and their SPYS badges broke. Myria, Techer and Wina fell to the ground. The two medical droids and Bop shattered to pieces outside the force shield. Wina howled to Evilzen.

Scientist 00123 regained his consciousness for a moment, and yelled, "Stoooooop! Don't hurt them!"

Wina summoned two big spiritual wolves to seize Scientist 00123 (Evilzen). They yanked onto both of his arms.

Evilzen (Scientist 00123) growled loudly, "You filthy dogs! Get away from me! You think that they can stop me? You foolish primitive life forms from nowhere in the universe! You think that you know everything; so ignorant! You know nothing about existence!"

Evilzen (Scientist 00123) tossed the two wolves away and summoned the planet to open up its energy core. It was like a black hole, sucking everything into it. Myria created an illusion and tried to distract Evilzen, while they tried to run away. Techer picked up the force shield and held it up to avoid falling into the core energy.

Scientist 00123 (Evilzen) snapped back into consciousness, "Run! I can't hold Evilzen any longer! Run! I am sorry, Wina!"

Then he forced himself to jump into the core energy of Unknown.

A loud voice boomed from the core energy, "You fool! We can rule this planet together! And those fools will become other Knowers! What have you done!"

Then, Unknown closed its core.

Wina, Myria and Techer lay on the ground. They felt fatigue, and they knew that they were infected by the virus, Disaster. They saw the soot and smoke disappear on the Knowers and their real faces revealed. Each of them were civilians from different planets. The one laying closest to

Myria wore a SPYS Star badge, and the name tag on his lab coat was Mr. Testi, the trainer. Myria was terrified and wanted to wake him up, but she was too weak to move. They were all imprisoned by Evilzen, the evil alter-ego of Scientist 00123.

Wina felt miserable, and she sobbed about Scientist 00123's sacrifice. Unknown was bright purple with solid ground, nothing was translucent anymore. But they were all dying.

6.

SUPERVIRUS

In the SPYS Star Control Room, Lady JJ watched I-Boy on the screen calling, "May-day! May-day!" She replayed the video stream again and again. Lady JJ tried to pick up a trace and hoped that she could locate the coordinates of I-Boy. Dr. Cherry BEE directed the commander droids to search for Unknown, as it suddenly disappeared.

Luca could not save them because it was impossible to open a portal without coordinates or when the subject was in motion.

Dr. Cherry BEE shouted, "Lady JJ, do your thing! Travel back in time and turn this whole Supernova Pandemic around! Save IMT and our missing scientists from Evilzen!"

Lady JJ replied, "I did travel back in time millions of times. I cannot remember all the happenings, but this is the best result."

Luca tried to reestablish the communication with the MediPod and the portable MediBay on Unknown. Suddenly, I-Boy appeared on the screen, and lost contact again. He seemed to be knocked out. His life sign was detected in a split second and disconnected again. The signal was unstable.

Luca reported that the MediPod had been located, and it was not in motion. Lady JJ and Dr. Cherry BEE were relieved to learn the news. Dr. Cherry BEE informed everyone in SPYS Star to take precautions, as they were bringing in a damaged MediPod that may be compromised by the virus. Everyone was instructed to activate their hazmat suits. In the control room, Lady JJ and Dr. Cherry BEE continued the search for Unknown.

Luca opened a portal at the SPYS Launching Bay and commanded Karini, the drone, to tow I-Boy's MediPod to the parking zone. I-Boy's MediPod was damaged with a few fissures on the screen. Two medical droids removed I-Boy from the MediPod and put him in a LifePod. He was unconscious and holding tight onto a bag of test tubes. Luca realized that those were the virus samples and the green matter that IMT collected from Unknown. He immediately sent the bag of test tubes to Dr. Cedric of the vaccine development department for analysis. I-Boy was then sent to the Medical Center for a thorough check-up, where all other medical team members had their check-ups after returning to SPYS Star.

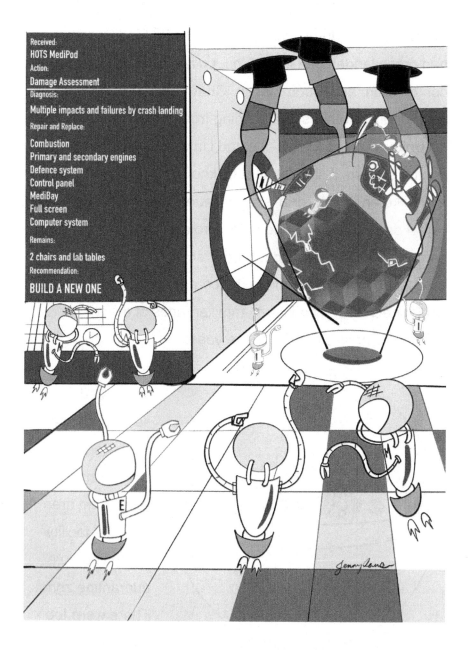

Received:
HOTS MediPod
Action:
Damage Assessment
Diagnosis:
Multiple impacts and failures by crash landing
Repair and Replace:
Combustion
Primary and secondary engines
Defence system
Control panel
MediBay
Full screen
Computer system
Remains:
2 chairs and lab tables
Recommendation:
BUILD A NEW ONE

Luca ordered the engineer droids to move I-Boy's MediPod to the repair center and conduct damage reports;

the same procedures were done on HOT's MediPod as it had crash landed on Green Lips. Luca went back to the control room and found that Dr. Cherry BEE and Lady JJ were dealing with a signal coming from the portable MediBay on Unknown. They finally located Unknown. According to the control system, it showed that Unknown is not a planet; it is more like an illusion or a 'space platform'. Luca re-coded the signal and reactivated one of the broken medical droid's cameras. It live streamed a horrific scene of bodies lying across the land. Everyone in the control room was shocked and speechless to see many familiar faces of the SPYS missing scientists after all these years.

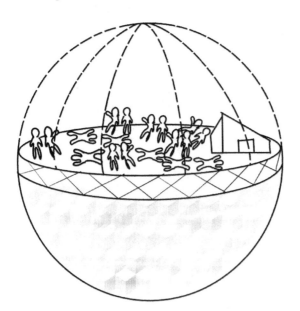

Lady JJ suggested sending a task force troop to Unknown to survey the area near the facility for setting up a quarantine zone. There were too many infected subjects. SPYS Star did not have the space nor the resources to treat them at SPYS Star.

Dr. Cherry BEE agreed, "We do not know a lot about the Disaster virus on Unknown yet. We should be careful before we intake all the subjects, while Dr. Cedric and his team are doing further research and experiment on each virus from Earth, Pinet, Green Lips and Unknown."

Dr. Cherry BEE called Dr. Crown to the control room, "Dr. Crown, your team is assigned to set up a quarantine zone on Unknown. It was revealed as a space platform created by Evilzen, disguised as a planet. IMT and many missing SPYS Star scientists were found infected by the virus and are in critical conditions. And please search for the green matter and check out its substances to see if they are useful."

Dr. Crown took a closer look at the infected subjects and the environment on the screen, "O.M.G. Those green matter seems like..." Dr. Crown was astonished.

Dr. Cherry BEE cleared her throat, "Ahem! Luca already prepared a task force troop and a MediPod for you. Your team will be leaving in five minutes. Godspeed and we will be in touch!"

Dr. Crown called her cat, Fuzzy, and gathered her team, then they left for Unknown.

Back at the Medical Center, Dr. Cedric in his hazmat suit checked I-Boy's life signs and the reports generated by the medical droids. The data showed that I-Boy was infected with the virus. I-Boy was concealed in a Lifepod and he was paralyzed. Dr. Cedric instructed the medical droids to draw blood from I-Boy for further virus analysis and cell testing. Then Dr. Cedric checked on the health condition of Team R, Team Medics United and HOTS. All of their life signs and reports show that they were healthy and no viruses were detected. They were all taking a good rest after their long mission in the lifePods.

Meanwhile Dr. Cherry BEE called on the P.A. for Dr. Cedric and his team to have an emergency meeting at the control room. He asked his two assistants, 2D Man and Miss GG, to upload the virus analysis of the four planets, the four virus samples and the experimental testing reports to the central system before attending the meeting. Then he uploaded the findings and the data of the green matter collected by IMT and the Pump Juice delivered by Team Medics United to the central system as well. He brought along both elements to the control room.

Dr. Cedric entered the control room and was overwhelmed by the loud and noisy conversation. Dr. Cherry BEE was talking with Dr. Crown face to face on a call. Dr. Cedric joined Lady JJ, Luca and the rest of his team at the meeting table watching the task force troop setting up an isolation center in the quarantine zone behind Dr. Crown. Dr. Cherry BEE realized everyone had arrived.

She informed everyone that Dr. Crown and her team were in charge of the quarantine zone next to the facility on the space platform, previously known as Unknown. They would put all the infected subjects, including IMT, into hibernation states.

Dr. Crown interrupted the briefing, "Excuse me, everyone! I need you to see this. We found one subject was conscious, lying next to IMT. She has a weak pulse and is mute. She used her telepathy to communicate with us. She asked us for help to put her back in the tank with the green matter, and I suspect that the green fluid is the energy drink from Earth. We need Dr. Cedric to confirm this. The space platform is falling apart. We don't have much time!"

Dr. Crown walked in the facility building showing a lot of advanced settings on the screen. She entered a room down the main hallway, inside had several huge incubators holding a still subject. Everyone was startled to see the scene, except for Dr. Cherry BEE. Dr Crown went up to one of the incubators with a girl floating in the illuminous green fluid.

Dr. Crown spoke again, "She is Wina. She has something to say to us. Luca, can you amplify her speech?"

Lady JJ and Cherry BEE recognized Wina right away, as she was on the video stream recorded by IMT earlier. Wina looked at Dr. Crown's face directly, and her face was shown on the screen, "There is no such need. I will use my telepathy to speak to your mind and you can all hear me well. Scientist 00123 left a message for Dr. Cherry BEE."

Everyone in the control room was murmuring.

Wina continued to speak on behalf of Scientist 00123, "Greeting to Dr. Cherry BEE and my fellows of SPYS Research Department. If Wina is delivering this message to you, I am properly not around anymore. And my brother's evil plan must have failed. Thank you for searching up for me in all these years. I carried out this classified project for 10 years; finally I completed experiment number 123. I created Wina. However, I was told to terminate her, and S.P.Y.S. Committee ceased all support for this project. So I found the green matter to keep the experiment and this space platform vitalized. However, the green matter is hard to buy from the drink company and was used up over time. I have no

choice but to bait on voyagers. I made a disguised planet 'Unknown' and attracted many SPYS scientists to explore here. I imprisoned and converted them into energy and fueled them with the green matter to support Wina and the space platform. Wina is the last hope to hold this space platform together. Once the green matter loses its illumination in the fluid of Wina's incubator, she will deactivate and the space platform will disappear.. The green matter will last for less than 24 hours. Please forgive me for all these."

Wina and Dr. Cherry BEE had a short private telepathic conversation after Scientist 00123's message. It was intense for everyone in the control room.

Dr. Crown then spoke up, "Dr. Cedric, please prepare a solution as soon as possible. My team and I had done an initial analysis on the virus samples of Proton and Kids Power Academy. They have the same DNA strands, although they appear in different forms. We concluded that they should be the same virus. Our reports were uploaded in the central system; I hope they can be useful for finding the cure. We do not have much time. We will try to keep all the infected subjects alive until the cure comes. Godspeed, we will talk again later." Dr. Crown ended the call.

Dr. Cherry BEE requested to hear the reports from the four medical teams. Dr. Cedric retrieved the footage and the virus reports from the systems and showed them on the screens. 2D Man and Miss GG explained the findings to everyone.

2D Man started, "Team R's footage about Earth showed that it has recently undergone a global pandemic of COVID-19. The virus hit them in several waves. The virus damaged the human's respiratory system and caused fibrosis of lungs and led to death. It was transmitted through big droplets. Team R recorded the mutated COVID-19 in India. It matches with the virus that the whole universe is suffering from, and we have run some tests on the virus sample to confirm the hypothesis."

Dr. Cedric interrupted, "I received a report from LG on Earth just now. It showed that the wild animals, creatures and marine habitants took sanctuary in nature from COVID-19. Nature protects its creations from contracting the virus. However, nature did not seem to protect humans in the pandemic. LG said she was still on the way to find Monty, and she will report on the condition of the domestic animals later on."

Lady JJ excused herself back to the control system panel after hearing LG's report. She needed to assist LG to find Monty as it had been two days since the mission took off.

Miss GG continued to explain the findings of Team Medics United, "There was toxic rain pouring on Pinet. The virus, Juice Bug, like tiny bubbles, was found in the rain. The Juice Bug virus caused fibrous hearts. PineKing created a formula to make Pump Juice which can slow down the symptoms caused by the virus but cannot neutralize the virus. Team Medics United collected some Pump Juice back to us. We are still confirming the effect on the virus."

2D Man then showed footage of Green Lips on the screen, he explained, "The virus, Stone Lips, turned Lipsy's lips into crystalized stone. HOTS found the tiny bubbles everywhere on Green Lips. Once the Lipsies were infected by the virus, tiny red dots would grow on their lips and burst out crystal spikes and cause them a great deal of pain. They lost their appetite and starved to death. A-Girl gave them some Pump Juice but it had no effect on Lipsies. It was a horrific scene. We compared the Stone Lips with other virus samples and found that they shared the same DNA strand."

Dr. Cedric then talked about the green matter, "As Wina had mentioned before, the green matter is no use on the virus. It is just the same fluid as Team R had brought back from Earth. Humans called them sport drinks or energy drinks. The main compounds are carbohydrates, sugar and protein. It cannot neutralize any virus. We are still working on Pump Juice and we think that it should be the key for developing the cure. We still need a bit of time to find the right solution. We conclude the findings below from all the virus samples:

1. They have the same DNA strands.
2. A tiny shiny red dot is contained in the microorganism
3. Causes fibrous organs, crystalized status and paralysis
4. Transmits by droplets and bubbles

"Those findings showed that they are the same virus. We officially named the virus, Brlingrr Brlingrr. We took the name from its appearance and the reflections of the red dot like a crystal, blinking from the inside. So far we knew that Pump Juice can slow down the development of the

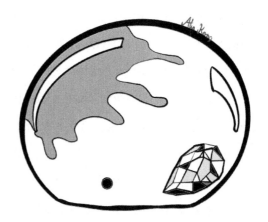

symptoms caused by Brlingrr Brlingrr. We have a very tight time frame to run more tests to confirm the Pump Juice has the key compound for the cure. If there are no further questions, please excuse us. We hope we can put the cure in a trial run in the next few hours."

Dr. Cedric and his team were dismissed.

Dr. Cherry BEE asked Luca to design a drone to disinfect the infected space, planets and stars. She asked him to put it into mass production as they need millions of them to cover the whole galaxy. Luca nodded and went to the mechanic center to start his work with the droids. Dr. Cherry BEE returned back to the control system panel and joined Lady JJ to work with Dr. Crown on an evacuation plan for receiving all the subjects back to SPYS Facility in the next 24 hours.

In the Infectious Virus Department Laboratory, Dr. Cedric was discussing with 2D Man and Miss GG about using messenger ribonucleic acid (mRNA) strands to develop a cure. The mRNA would give instructions to the host's body to create a protein of Brlingrr Brlingrr. The protein of Brlingrr Brlingrr that is set in the body would trigger the immune system to send T lymphocytes to kill the virus. 2D Man also mentioned that using mRNA strands could shorten more than half of the development time. They agreed time was crucial and immediately started the process.

The analysis of the Pump Juice prepared by the medical droids showed that it consisted of new acidic compounds that could be the key components for neutralizing the virus. Dr. Cedric instructed 2D Man and Miss GG to adjust the pH level of the compounds multiple times and tested them on Brlingrr Brlingrr. These were the results:

pH Level	Neutralize Brlingrr Brlingrr	Side effect	Fatality
1-3	100%	100%	80-100%
4-5	100%	50-70%	30-50%
6	100%	2%	0.5%
>7	0%	0%	0%

Miss GG explained the findings: if the new Pump Juice compound were unusually acidic, it could neutralize any microscopic germs, bacterias and viruses below pH 6. The compound at pH below 3 killed the membrane of Brlingrr Brlingrr that protected the core cell of the virus, however, it was extremely harmful to all life-forms. If the new compound is acidic concentrated, then the fatality rate is high. Dr. Cedric asked 2D Man and Miss GG to adjust the compound to pH 6 as it would be safe to use on infected subjects.

The team followed Dr. Cedric's instruction to create a trial cure and test it on I-Boy, as he was infected with Brlingrr Brlingrr. I-Boy responded to the cure immediately. His blood test showed that the virus in his body was disappearing. And his life signs indicated that he was regaining health. Dr. Cedric reported the results to Dr. Cherry BEE. Dr. Cherry BEE asked Luca to put the trial cure into production for more testing on the infected subjects at the four epicenters: Earth, Pinet, Green Lips and the quarantine zone at Unknown.

While I-Boy was recovering in his LifePod, the other three medical teams were refreshed with good sleep. They were ready to deliver the cure to their assigned designations. 2D Man informed Luca they had the disinfectants ready to test on the four planets. Then Luca unveiled his Tubweques, the new spray-craft he created. He commanded the droids to load the disinfectant into three Tubweques. The three medical teams piloted them off to Earth, Pinet and Green Lips.

Luca then opened a portal to the space platform at Unknown to meet with Dr. Crown and deliver the cure to her for a trial run on the infected subjects. Luca also brought a Tubweque with him to disinfect the area. Everything seemed to be in order and S.P.Y.S. Committee was ready to put the cure into mass production for all infected life forms throughout the universe.

A few hours later, the three medical teams and Dr. Crown reported to the control room that they had injected the cure in all the infected subjects and all of them seemed to be recovering. They disinfected their assigned designations, and no more Brlingrr Brlingrr could be detected.

Suddenly, I-Boy's LifePod triggered the alarm. Dr. Cedric and his team rushed to the Medical Center and found that I-Boy's life signs were chaotic and he had a high fever. Dr. Cedric drew blood from I-Boy and the droids conducted a thorough analysis. I-Boy was infected by Brlingrr Brlingrr aggressively, but they could not detect any virus in his blood cells. Dr. Cedric and Dr. Cherry BEE were shocked. They went blank.

Then the control room received a S.O.S. from Dr. Crown, and another S.O.S. from Pinet, and then from Green Lips and then Earth.

I-Boy was in a critical condition. Dr. Cedric put him in hibernation right away.

7.
MEET MONTY

Back on Earth…

LG had parted from Team R three days ago to find Monty. She missed her home planet, Earth, and seldom visited her friends ever since she had attended Kids Power Academy. Her family moved to the space station, and they were evacuated to SPYS Star since the pandemic began. LG was glad that her family is safe and healthy. She knew finding Monty on Earth had given her a great opportunity to revisit her friends again.

She went astray to check on her friends at her favourite Chinese school. She still remembered the emblem of the school, the symbol of 'Yin and Yang'. 'Yin' represents the dark and 'Yang' is the light. Together, they are the most powerful elements forming harmony and balance throughout the universe. LG toured the school campus again to refresh the-good-old times with her friends. The school was rather empty, and no happiness filled the air anymore. All the students put on masks and practiced physical distancing. There was no expression on everybody's face.

"The atmosphere is depressing..." LG exclaimed in her head.

There were great changes in the living style during the pandemic on Earth. There were news broadcasts on the mutation of the virus COVID-19. The WHO suggested a set of hygiene regimes for humans to follow to avoid contracting the virus which were similar to the ones that S.P.Y.S. Committee had suggested. COVID-19 brought along raging numbers of casualties and fatalities and the collapses of healthcare and economic systems in many countries. International travelling was banned, and gatherings were restricted. Several pharmaceutical companies developed and rolled out their own vaccines in most of the countries, but none of the vaccines can 100% neutralize COVID-19. And the virus has mutated even stronger and transmitted more aggressively.

"I guess humans need to stick with the set of hygiene regimes for a bit longer. Masks covering saliva and droplets are the most effective way to avoid contracting the virus!" LG thought out loud and was observing the environment.

The bright side of the pandemic is that nature was healing. Humans loved to spend more time with their families at home. They stayed within their own bubbles to continue their own living. Factories and commercial businesses were mostly closed, which led to less environmental pollution. The

COVID-19 pandemic made humans understand that they were destroying their own home. The ozone layer was healing and the atmosphere was cleared from smog. The global warming rate was slowing down. Humans learned about nature all over again.

LG was surprised, "This COVID-19 is not all bad after all! It is actually doing well to the Earth!"

While LG was still enjoying her hometown, a head with massive red hair popped right in front of LG's screen.

It was Lady JJ's holocall, "LG! Where are you! What are you doing at your old school?! Where is Monty?! We are facing catastrophes here! I need you to find Monty now! Blah blah blah blah...."

Lady JJ babbled on and on... The camera on LG's hazmat suit was livestreaming to the SPYS control system. Lady JJ and the S.P.Y.S. Committee were monitoring everyone in their mission.

LG was startled, "Um--mm... Wh--at? What--- you say--- the con---t--ion is ---rea---lly ---- he--re!" LG was faking a bad reception to avoid Lady JJ's tantrum.

Lady JJ raised her voice, "Have you found Monty yet? He must have left some trace since he knows you are coming for him. According to Dr Cedic, you said that most of the wild animals in the Safaris were not infected by COVID-

19, and no unknown virus was detected on them. Please find out the condition of domestic pets in the cities"

LG nodded, "Roger that. Will keep you posted." And she ended the call.

LG used her smart glasses to search for Monty. However, there was no result. Then she uploaded pictures of Monty into Amal, an artificial intelligent robot resembling an outfit for LG. Amal could not locate Monty either. Yet, she showed the gooey slimes that were found everywhere on the streets.

LG questioned, "What are those? I cannot see them anywhere."

Amal spoke out, "Those were undetectable dog's snot, which matches the snot on the pictures. You cannot see them with your bare eyes. I reveal them by analyzing the data and calculating the variables of the surroundings. I think they may be clues to find Monty."

LG gave it a thought and asked Amal to run a DNA test on the snot including boogers and nostril hair. The report confirmed that it matches the DNA of the schnauzer. LG knew that she was close to Monty. She blasted off into the air and circled around a few blocks.

Amal notified LG about the 'snot message' on every street, and read to her, "'DogTech SuXxxx x*###' in L.A." Amal added, "The last two words were not clear!"

LG knew she was running out of time. She asked Amal to search for the closest result and lock on the location and set on autopilot to take her there.

She landed on a huge blue cuboids building with a dome roof. It carried a sizable signage with 'DogTech Supplies Supermarket' written on it.

LG stared at it and was confused, "Amal, are you sure?"

Before Amal could answer, a holocall came in showing Lady JJ's smiling face on her screen, "Good, you've found Monty! Please give him the green box, Luca embedded a special translator on the badge. You will be able to communicate with Monty, the Superdetective!"

LG puzzled, "This is a pet supplies supermarket. It does not look like any dog shelter!"

Lady JJ continued, "Sometimes, things are not what they seem. We have serious issues to deal with here at SPYS. I've got to go, we will talk again soon." Lady JJ then ended the call.

While LG was still putting the pieces together, a small gray schnauzer with a big round stuffy nose stuck its head out from a side door and barked at her. It stared at her with his soulful eyes like it was trying to signal a message to her.

"Ruff ruff!!"

LG was curious and went closer to the cute little schnauzer. She patted it and praised its great tricks of standing on its two hind legs. "Good job, little fellow! What's wrong with you? You have a bit of a stuffy nose, you caught a cold? I like your little blanket, looks like a Sherlock's style raincoat!" She picked up the schnauzer and gave it a squeezy hug.

The dog kicked out of LG's grasp quickly, then bit on LG's boots and pulled her in the ally. He barked loudly this time, "Agrrrrrrrrrrruff! Ruff!"

LG almost lost her balance, but she managed to stand back on her feet. "Wait! What is it?"

They were in the backyard of the DogTech Supplies Supermarket. It turned out that it was a secret entrance of a DogTech Agent Center. It opened as a supermarket in disguise during daytime. Amal showed a list of data on LG's smart glasses confirming the dog was Monty!

LG talked softly to Amal, "But, he is nothing like the Monty in the picture. The picture shows that Monty is a handsome, strong, good-size dog. I guess photo-making apps

are overly abused these days! Lady JJ should have cross-checked the reference before uploading this photo to me." She finished talking with Amal and turned around to the cute small gray dog.

"Monty! Wow! You were the one that sent us a hologram message about Earth. You are much smaller in person though." LG cried.

And Monty barked affirmatively, "Ruff! Ruff!"

"I am the Lightning Girl, or LG for short. Lady JJ sent me here to give this to you." LG handed over a green box to Monty.

He opened the box and took out a KPA (Kids Power Academy) Superdetective Badge. It has the shape of a star with bold lettering, "KPA", which beamed in gold. The badge was equipped with an advanced translator that can translate all animals' languages into other languages in the universe. It also included a life support system, a hazmat suit device, a live camera, an AR, a holocall system and more. He pinned it onto his 'Sherlock cape' and wiggled his ears. LG helped him to do the setting, activated all the systems on the badge including the hazmat suit and translation devices. Monty felt so proud to achieve this honorable badge and earn the title of Superdetective. Monty did a 'moonwalker' dance on his hind legs and howled happily followed by a, 'Blesss--choo', wetty sneeze.

Monty spoke in a deep low voice, emphasizing he was taking care of things seriously, "Excuse me! Hello LG! Lady JJ updated us about the virus, Brlingrr Brlingrr, spreading all over the whole universe, and S.P.Y.S. Committee just released the first batch of vaccines two days ago to Earth, Pinet, Green Lips and Unknown. Things seemed to finally fall into the right place, but-- thi-s.. mor--nin-- Bllesss-Chooll!! Oh, excuse me! I have had this long lasting allergy since I was vaccinated. Because of this allergy, I halted the vaccination on my troops and reported this to Lady JJ."

LG was terrified, yet felt fascinated about the side effect of the vaccine on Monty. She said, "Yes I heard about the vaccines, but then I don't have any more news. And do you mind if I ask Amal to do a full scan on you?"

Monty winked his eyes and gave a 'no' ruff.

Amal scanned Monty with the device embedded in LG's smart glasses. While Monty led the way into the DogTech Agent Center, LG commanded

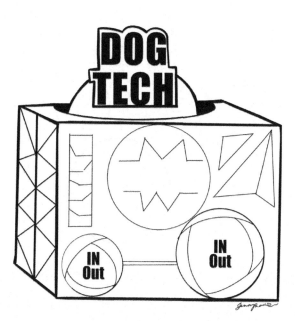

Amal to conduct analysis of Monty's health conditions and sent the report back to the SPYS Control system for Dr. Cedric.

Monty accessed a hidden door on the wall of the building with his paw print, and they entered an open field. LG saw all the dogs were dressed in specially made PPE with a round helmet like an astronaut suit, covering their whole bodies from their snouts to their paws. They were divided into groups and attended different training sessions, such as biting on targets, shooting darts, practicing ninja-escapes, etc.

Every dog that passed by Monty, gave him a solute, and barked, "Ruff ruff!"

Peter

LG was impressed, "Monty, you must be a very respectable leader and must have done great things!"

Monty was troubled with his stuffy nose and could not reply in time. Another dog in PPE came by, saluting Monty. Then a third dog did the same thing, and he began to speak, "Monty is our great hero. He is our role model of being a human's best companion!"

LG was surprised she could understand a dog's language, "How can you speak a human's language?"

The third dog continued, "Luca sent us these PPE this morning. He instructed us to put them on right away! He told us that the first batch of vaccines failed. He fetched me to find Monty, and Lady JJ will have an announcement for us soon. By the way, I am Peter."

As Monty and LG were about to rush back to the DogTech Main Center, Peter bragged on, "If you want to know more about Monty's great things, read his book, *Montgomery Schnauzer P.I.* written by Mr. Timothy Forner! His story will blow your min–"

Monty cut off Peter's conversation, "Thank you for the introduction, let's get to the Main Center. We have more important things to deal with."

Peter parted and went back to his training on peeing on the lamp pole to leave secret code messages.

LG saw everything and was disgusted about those practices. She wanted to get her mind off the scene, and stepped aside to take some fresh air. Monty waved at her and asked her to stay close. They entered a red door and took an elevator up the top floor and arrived at the Main Center. It was a huge operation room which took up the entire floor. The whole premise was connected with computers, machines, systems, monitors, screens and more, like a totally technologically enhanced system control base. There were over fifty dog agents working there. Monty and LG heard a familiar voice yelling and screaming not far away. Then they saw Lady JJ's face on the biggest screen in the center of the room.

Lady JJ spotted LG and Monty's arrival at the Main Center and raised her voice, "What took you two so long? We have a serious problem. The vaccine and the disinfectants that we developed failed us. We received S.O.S messages from Pinet, Green Lips, Unknown and your planet, Earth. The local civilians of those planets who took the vaccine felt better for the first few hours, and the Brlingrr

Brlingrr virus seems to be disappearing in the hosts' bodies. However, everything went south after a day.

"The crystal spikes actively bursted out from the hosts' bodies and many of them are in critical conditions now. The S.O.S messages also mentioned that they sprayed disinfectant everywhere on their own planets, and no Brlingrr Brlingrr virus was detected after that. However, the local civilians seemed to contract the virus much faster than before. There are many uncertainties and unknowns about this virus. We thought we neutralized it. Instead it is still haunting us, yet more aggressively. We are working on every possibility here."

LG and Monty were speechless; they kept silent and waited for further instructions from Lady JJ. She commanded, "Originally, I gave both of you a mission to investigate the nature of Earth, as it is not infected by virus, in fact it was healed by the virus. LG reported to Dr Cedric earlier showing that nature was protecting its creations. And we just ran more tests and analysis on the report of Monty's allergy conditions, and it seemed like the vaccine had a reaction on COVID-19 (Brlingrr Brlingrr virus). We were not sure until we could run a thorough test on Monty. But we are affirmative that Monty is infected and carrying the mutated COVID-19 (Brlingrr Brlingrr virus). So please have the hazmat suit on all the time and take precautions.   We also tested a hypothesis on domestic pets contracting the mutated COVID-19. They have a very high chance of suffering from the failure of their respiratory system and fibrous lungs, like most of the humans do. So I asked Luca to deliver PPE for the dog agents this morning."

Lady JJ cleared her voice and continued, "So, your new mission is to collect the latest virus samples and information in the three epicenters, Earth, Pinet, and Green Lips. Dr. Crown is working on the virus sample on Unknown. So it has been taken care of. Monty will use his supertrace snot to collect the data and information for us. LG, your job is to assist Monty and his troop to complete the mission. Please command Amal to teleport the team to each destination. You have three hours."

Before LG and Monty could respond, Lady JJ ended the call.

Monty spoke directly to LG, "Before we go on the mission, I need to be clear with you. I am not a hugger, so please don't give me a squeeze hug again! Bless-- Choo!" Monty's symptoms became worse than before.

"OK! I get it. Seriously, are you OK?" LG was concerned about Monty's condition.

Monty sniffled loudly trying to suck back all his snot inside his nose, "I am OK, just ever since I had the vaccine, I felt so fatigued with this allergy. I need to get a good sleep after all! But I have a question about the hazmat suit. You see, I have some special skills. My supertrace snot is undetectable. I usually sneeze out and spit them everywhere on the street for collecting data like chemical compounds, viruses, microorganisms and particles for analysis. I can even leave secret messages to my agents without anyone noticing them."

LG felt gross about the snot thingy and gave a blank face to Monty.

Monty ignored her and continued, "My concern is would the hazmat suit restrict my ability to sneeze out supertrace snot?"

LG was disgusted, she stuck out her tongue, "Time out! I cannot stand it, it's too gross. And is it necessary for you to sneeze them everywhere?"

Monty looked at her with his soulful eyes. LG was sort of hypnotized by his cute stare and she surrendered, "Alright, just don't let me know a thing. And the hazmat suit is the most innovative filter 'shield' invented by Luca. It acts as a microorganism barrier wrapping the user inside, preventing any viruses or germs from being in contact. It is a one-way barrier; no germs or bacteria come in but everything can go out. "

Monty was amazed and said to LG, "You don't have to worry about my supertrace snot. You will not even notice it! Besides, this allergy gave me an advantage to make massive sneezes, so my supertrace snot can cover infinite areas each time."

Monty then turned around and summoned two troopers over. They would be in disguise as domestic pets to collect the undetectable snot, because Monty did not want to provoke the humans. One trooper would collect Monty's supertrace snot on Earth. The other trooper followed Monty and LG to other epicenters.

A dog, with a name tag 'General Bonechewer' written on it, approached Monty and asked him to look at a big machine on the other side of the Main Center. LG followed them and recognized the machine must have been sent by Luca. It looked like a big juicer.

"What is this?" LG was curious.

Monty explained, "This is a decomposer of my supertrace snot. It is also called a booger juicer."

LG almost fainted, "OK, that's enough; can we go now?"

Monty asked LG to give him another minute to explain the whole operation of the booger juicer to General Bonechewer. LG overheard their conversation about dumping all the supertrace snot into the machine once the troop collected it. Then it would spin to drain out all the moisture of the snot and leave a hard residue.

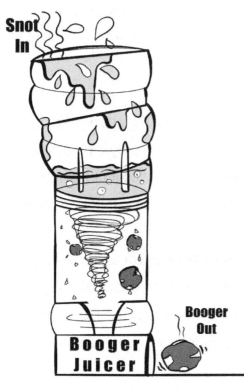

Monty told General Bonechewer to carefully put the residue in a box in a dry place at a temperature of 20 degrees celsius. If the temperature ran over or the residue became moist again, Luca could not download the data of the virus from it.

LG could not take the picture out of her head and whined, "One Dragon Boy is full of poop, now I have Monty, and he is full of boogers! Someone, help me please!!"

"BLESSS-CHOOOOO!" Monty made a thunderous sneeze. This time, his snot was everywhere, flooding the whole building, "Excuse me! I can't help it!"

LG was lucky to have her hazmat suit on, no germs or microparticles could break through the device. But she was still disgusted, "We must finish this quickly and get you to the MediBay of SPYS Star. Your nose blows up like a red ball. We need to go now!"

Monty rubbed his nose, "Yes. My trooper and I will bring along a snot sucker. It will help to collect my supertrace snot at the other epicenters!"

LG nodded and asked Monty to prepare a spacecraft to meet at the open field. General Bonechewer ordered all the dog agents to carry an elastic pocket. It was a device sent by Luca that allows the dog agents to upload anything to the 'bone', like a drive, and they can retrieve it from the elastic pocket. General Bonechewer instructed them to upload their jars filled with yellow fluid for indicating the undetectable supertrace snot to the 'bone', so they could be retrieved on the mission.

LG went to the open field to wait for Monty. The sun was setting. She then holocalled Team R to check in with them. They returned to Earth two days ago to assist in the first batch of vaccinations for humans. However, the vaccine from SPYS could not neutralize COVID-19 (Brlingrr Brlingrr) virus; instead, the vaccinated humans suffered from more aggressive symptoms. LG informed them that she and Monty would do further investigations on other epicenters and report back to the S.P.Y.S. Committee. They would endeavour to create a successful vaccine. LG told them to hang in there for a bit longer. S.P.Y.S. Committee would send help to them very soon. Team R was encouraged by LG's words; they had been working day and night to take care of the vaccinated humans who showed severe symptoms again.

Suddenly, the ground was shaking; something big rose up behind LG. She immediately turned around, but could not see anything clearly because the light was rather dim. She saw a huge shadow with one long arm stretched out, trying to grab her. She was not ready for this.

She braced and cried loudly, "Whaaaaaaaat Ahh!"

All the spotlights turned on around the field, and the cries got the attention of every dog agent.

Monty broke the silence and called, "LG, LG, our spacecraft is ready; welcome aboard. I am sorry. I should give you a heads-up about it."

Every dog agent was still staring at LG.

"All agents, back to work now!" Monty ordered firmly.

LG slowly got up and gasped, she looked around and saw a broken airplane with only one wing. It was repainted in blue, with a DogTech Agent signage on it. She did not understand.

She flew to Monty and asked, "Why a broken airplane?!"

Monty explained, "Since the pandemic, many airplanes were abandoned because there is no more international traveling. So we got this plane from the airplane graveyard. We tried to convert it into a spacecraft, it's halfway done, and the engine is still working."

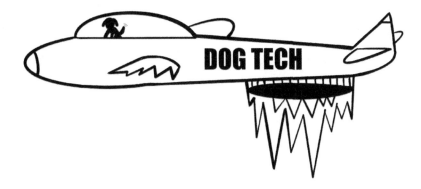

LG was annoyed, "You fly this with one wing?!"

Monty responded proudly, "Don't worry, we installed a powerful thruster!"

LG rolled her eyes, "How do you balance the plane with one wing?!"

Monty sheepishly said, "Oops... We didn't think about that."

LG sighed and went straight to the cockpit, and Monty followed her. Peter, the dog who met LG before, closed the door of the 'spacecraft' and ordered the troop to fasten the seatbelts to get ready for takeoff. In the cockpit, LG and Monty sat at the captain's seats. While LG took a small device from her outfit and inserted it into the control panel, Monty holocalled Lady JJ.

LG spoke up, "Lady JJ, Amal is ready to teleport us to Pinet! Please inform Pineking we will be meeting him in two minutes."

8.
DISASTER ZONES

In a blink of an eye, the spacecraft landed right in front of Pineking, where he was sitting on his throne doing nothing.

Pineking was so surprised, "What?! I just got off the holophone with my mom. And it is not even two minutes yet!"

Everyone got off the 'spacecraft' and LG marched to Pineking to greet him, "How are you doing? Seriously, just sit there and lock yourself in this castle?! Where is our Team Medics United?"

Pineking stood up from his throne and cried, "It's horrible out there! The vaccinated Pinenions have gone crazy, rolling around, biting anything they see!" Pineking sobbed, "The Team Medics United was at their medical station next to my castle, distributing my Pump Juice, which can slow down their aggressive and destructive behaviour. I am still working on a new formula of Pump Juice to totally suppress the symptoms caused by the Blringrr Blringrr virus. I just need to run the final test on the formula. The current formula of the Pump Juice can only freeze the virus for a short period of time."

LG introduced Monty, the Superdetective, to Pineking. She told Pineking that Monty needed to cover Pinet with his supertrace snot.

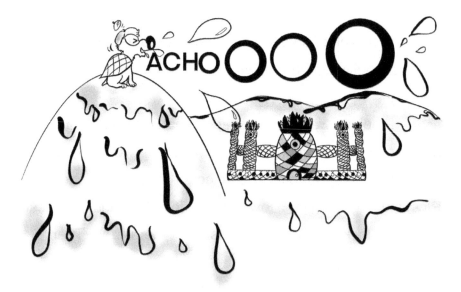

Pineking shuddered and gasped, "Nooo way…"

LG ignored his reaction and said, "We don't have a solution, yet Monty's supertrace snot will find us the answer. Now, if you'd please excuse us, Monty needs to go out and make a few thunderous, watery, slimy, smelly, gooey, boogery sneezes. But don't worry, according to Amal, they are undetectable except for the slime, booger and nasal hair. You will feel nothing about this!"

Pineking raged with anger, "No dog snot is going to take over my Pinet!"

LG pushed Pineking away, "OK! OK! We are going to clean it up, that's what the dog troops are here for, and they brought along a super powerful snot sucker to speed things up!"

While Pineking and LG were still chit-chatting, Monty already took the troops out to the field. He sneezed alarmingly. Pineking was so worried and rushed out his castle before LG could remind Pineking to put his hazmat suit on.

Pineking opened the door and was almost splattered with snot. Fortunately Dragoo wrapped him with its wings in time to avoid the goo.

LG caught up with Pineking at the main gate and was relieved, "Phew! That was close!"

LG and Pineking saw a disgusting, yet magnificent scene: Monty's supertrace snot was flooded everywhere beyond the horizon.

Pineking was sweating, "This is horribly disgusting."

LG nodded and agreed. Monty approached them and explained to the Pineking about the power of his supertrace snot. The troops were on the move to collect every single drop of Monty's supertrace snot into jars. Peter operated the

snot sucker, sweeping across the land, sucking the snot in a massive scale.

Monty suddenly howled loudly, "Incoming! Incoming! I heard three lifeforms storming our way!"

LG asked Amal to identify the threats.

Amal showed the result on LG's smart glasses and spoke, "They are the scientists of SPYS Star, one of the medical teams, Team Medics United. They seem to be very angry approaching us! Please prepare to 'fight' with your friends and the fatality is you may lose your BFF."

LG replied, "Amal, you are full of nonsense"

After Amal was dismissed, three zombie-like scientists appeared right in front of them.

Monty was scared, "Wh-o-o ar-e y-ou? Don't bite me!"

Smiling had a zombie-like face, she looked so tired and spoke first, "We are Team Medics United. What are you guys doing here!!!! We worked day and night and now you cover us with this gooey snot?!"

Little Porter added on, "Don't we have enough trouble already!"

Pineking felt sorry, "Sorry, I should have let you guys know earlier, so you can prepare for this. Monty is the Superdetective, and he is here to find an answer about the failure of the vaccine. This gooey thing is his undetectable supertrace snot for collecting the data and information about the virus."

Naky couldn't hold her anger anymore; she was soaked wet with the snot. "You call this undetectable snot! Look at me!!! This is–"

Monty interrupted Naky and ordered Peter to use the snot sucker to dry the team. After that, Monty ordered the troop to go to the other side to collect the snot and clean up the medical station.

Pineking invited everyone inside the castle. The Team Medic United stated their purpose of coming was to collect more Pump Juice to treat the Pinenions. They told Pineking that one-third of the Pinenions were treated; they seemed to calm down and were doing meditation. But they still needed to treat thousands of other Pinenions out there. The whole team was so exhausted treating the Pinenions nonstop, and they had not slept for two whole days. Smiling informed them that they could not hold on any longer. LG noticed the urgency of the situation. She told the team to have faith; S.P.Y.S. Committee would find a solution very soon.

Pineking notified everyone that the new formula of the Pump Juice was in the final stage of testing. Then he would go to SPYS Star to work with Dr. Cedric in the next few hours. Team Medics United farewelled, wished everyone best of luck and returned back to their station after getting more Pump Juice. LG, Monty and his troops collected all the supertrace snot and said farewell to Pineking. They returned back to their 'spacecraft' and were ready to go to Green Lips.

LG commanded Amal, "Take us to Green Lips!"

They arrived at Green Lips in a swift and saw a horrible stony scene of the planet, but no sign of Blringrr Blringrr virus was detected. All the Lipsies had become crystal statues. Monty and his troop got off the 'spacecraft' and scattered. They sniffed and examined each crystal statue.

Monty announced, "Alright! Let's all leave a mark at each crystal statue, treat them like a lampole and you know what to do! On my count, three, two, one, let's pee to leave a mark!"

The troop was literally peeing on the crystal statues. LG was speechless and twitched her eyebrows. The medical team, HOTS, were rushing towards them in concern from their medical base.

Minacko shouted loudly, "Stop! Stop!" A-Girl continued, "Why are you peeing on the Lipsies?! They are our patients and still conscious. They can see and hear you, but not for long..."

LG was relieved that someone stopped Monty and his troops in time before it turned into an extremely hilarious scene. She said, "We are so sorry. This is Monty, the Superdetective. We were sent by Lady JJ to investigate the vaccine and the virus. Monty will use his supertrace snot to trace the cause of the virus and the missing piece of the vaccine."

A-Girl replied directly, "S.P.Y.S. Committee already informed us that you guys were coming. We have a very sad and difficult situation here, the vaccinated Lipsy developed the same symptoms, but even faster and more aggressively than before. I tried to treat them with the leftover Pump Juice that I took from Pineking before I came to Green Lips. It slowed down the progress of the symptoms a little bit, but it won't help for long. They are dying, the crystal statues are the last stage of their lives. And I don't have much of the juice left."

Monty walked slowly to A-Girl and apologized, "I am sorry. This is sort of our dog agent's thingy. We were trained to pee whenever we see a lampole, a statue, a tree, et cetera to leave our secret marks and messages there. I'll waste no more time and get to work right now to find an answer for this universal problem.

LG then said to Team HOTS, "Let's go to your medical base, shall we?"

146

Monty stood on high ground and made a few roaring sneezes. This time, his sneeze was louder and gooier than before. His supertrace snot covered all the statues and flooded the upper lip of the planet. His troop was collecting the snot in jars; and Peter vacuumed the snot with the Snot Sucker.

While Monty and his troop were busy on their mission, LG was waiting for them at Team HOTS medical base and saw LipsK and LipsQ.

A-Girl spoke first, "We were lucky to halt the vaccine in time. Both LipsK and LipsQ did not take the vaccine, but they were infected from the very beginning. You visited them through the Wishing Tree's passage; they were already infected by the Brlingrr Brlingrr virus back then. I treated them with Pump Juice It worked better on them than the vaccinated Lipsies."

LG took a good look at LipsK and LipsQ, they were lying on the couch. Their lips had already turned into crystal.

LipsK pleaded LG in a raspy voice, "H-he-lp -u-s plea-se..."

LG comforted LipsK and everyone, "Just hang in there, we are trying to get a solution. Pineking is also working on a new formula of Pump Juice."

Just then, Monty interrupted and knocked on the door. Blobman opened the door. Monty entered and he spoke, "We gathered all the snot and we are ready to go."

LG saw the troop was returning to the 'spacecraft', and she finished off her words with Team HOTS and LipsK and Q, "Everyone stay strong, we will find a solution and S.P.Y.S. Committee will come to help very soon."

Then everyone nodded their heads firmly and farewell to each other.

Right before LG commanded Amal to teleport their spacecraft to Unknown, Lady JJ holocalled them, "LG and Monty, have you finished the mission on Pinet and Green Lips? Did you collect the information about the vaccine and the virus with your supertrace snot?"

LG replied promptly, "Yes, we have. We are about to go to Unknown."

Lady JJ was glad to hear that the mission was completed. She explained the situation of Unknown to LG and Monty, "Unknown, has been converted into SPYS Isolation Center. It is actually a space platform created by Evilzen and is not stable. Our team IMT was infected by the Brlingrr Brlingrr virus during the battle with Evilzen. He and his twin brother ended up swallowed by the core energy. We lost the coordinates of Unknown once; lucky that Luca managed to reactivate IMT's life support system and could locate the coordinates of this space platform. Once we made the first contact after the battle, we found all the missing SPYS Star's scientists on the space platform."

"When we found them, they were all unconscious and vomiting crystal powder. Luca helped Dr Crown and her team to set up an isolation center there. They took the first batch of vaccines to the SPYS Isolation Center and vaccinated everyone. However, same as Pinet, Green Lips and Earth, the vaccinated life forms were suffering from severe symptoms. Their lives are on the line, and the planet is not stable. It will disappear in a matter of time. We are closely working with Dr. Crown and got the necessary virus samples."

"I need you two to return to SPYS Star immediately and bring the troop. And please keep your hazmat suit on when you arrive, because the Brlingrr Brlingrr virus is now undetectable. We need to take extra precaution, even on SPYS Star." Then Lady JJ ended the call.

LG instructed Amal to go to SPYS Star.

9.
MONTY'S
INVESTIGATION

Amal teleported the 'spacecraft' to SPYS Star
launching bay. Luca was already there waiting for them. He
told LG to meet with Dr Cherry BEE, Lady JJ, Pineking and
the rest of the team at the SPYS Star Control Room. He then
asked Monty and the dog troops to follow him to a second
operation theatre where the booger juicer and Monty's
supertrace snot from Earth were in place. Luca had opened
a portal earlier to bring them back from the DogTech Agent
Center on Earth.

The booger juicer already finished making the residue
from Monty's supertrace snot on Earth. The residue was
basically a super-duper, big, dry, booger ball. Luca would
retrieve the data of chemical compounds, DNA,
microorganism and other elements regarding the virus and
the first vaccine from this Earth booger ball. While Luca was
busy on the analysis, Monty operated the booger juicer on
his supertrace snot that they had collected from Pinct and

Green Lips. Monty was groggy and almost fell asleep a few times. Peter gave him a 'chewy' to keep him awake. Monty shook off his weariness and continued to work the booger juicer. It was very efficient, only taking several minutes to generate the Pinet booger ball and the Green Lips booger ball. Luca repeated the same analysis on them as he did on the Earth booger ball. All three results showed positive on Brlingrr Brlingrr virus, but no antibodies of the vaccine were found in all three booger balls, because the virus had neutralized them all.

A call came through on the P.A. system from Lady JJ, "Luca and Monty please come to the control room. Please bring the reports and the three booger balls along!"

In the control room, Dr Cherry BEE, Lady JJ, LG and Pineking were working with S.P.Y.S. Committee to monitor and respond to the four medical teams in the field. Team R was taking care of the vaccinated humans who were suffering from the failure of their respiratory system. Team Medics United was treating the insane Pinenions. HOTS was waiting for UBER to deliver a new vaccine to save the Lipisies who had turned into crystal statues. And IMT was down, staying with other missing SPYS's scientists under the care of Dr. Crown at the Isolation Center. There were over twenty screens and all of them showed depressing, horrible footage. Everyone watched them with a heavy heart.

Dr. Cherry BEE talked softly to her son, "I hope your new formula of Pump Juice can be of great use."

Pineking finished the new formula of the Pump Juice and gave it to Dr.Cedric and his team to study it.

When Monty and Luca entered the control room, Lady JJ noticed Monty was very tired. He was wobbling and his eyelids drooped down halfway like he was about to fall asleep.

Lady JJ quickly approached Monty and picked him up, "What happened to you, Monty? You look awful!"

Monty sneezed right at Lady JJ's face, "Ahhhhh-Chooooo!!"

Lady JJ roared, "Tissue! Towel! Paper towels! Whatever! Anything!! Hurry!"

LG quickly took Monty away from Lady JJ and settled him on a couch with a blankie.

Lady JJ was covered with Monty's snot and shrieked, "Luca!!!!! What happened?! You said that nothing can go through this shield. So what happened now?! Am I infected?!"

Pineking gave Lady JJ a big towel to scrape off the snot on her face.

Luca sighed, "I told you a million times, that this is a hazmat suit not a shield! It is a filter that acts as a barrier to prevent bacteria and viruses from coming in contact with you, so you won't get infected. Anything that comes in contact with you is free of microorganisms. The goo on your face is just yucky gloop."

Luca took out a super powerful blow-dryer to dry up Lady JJ's fountain-like hair.

Dr. Cherry BEE commented, "When are you going to remember things?!"

Monty kept on sneezing and finally he caught his breath, "I need to use my nano senses to find the truth behind this case!"

He took off the blanket and walked slowly to the meeting table where Luca had already placed the three booger balls there. Everyone followed Monty to the meeting table and was expecting to see the century's greatest demonstration. LG was worried about Monty and stood right next to him, as he was still wobbling. The three booger balls were in different colors, and they did not have any awkward smell. They were each the size of a salad bowl. 'Earth' booger ball was green and brown. 'Pinet' booger ball was yellow. And 'Green Lips' booger ball was yellow green.

Monty went up on the table and began his demonstration. He held the Earth booger ball in his paws and gave it a sniff. Then a second sniff, then again and again more sniffs. Monty sniffed so heavily on the booger ball that his snout almost ran right into it.

He raised his head and said, "I cannot smell anything, the illness made me lose my smelling sense. I have no choice but to taste them. If you find this disturbing, you may take your leave now."

Monty's announcement drew even more attention from everyone of SPYS Star Facility. They broadcasted Monty's demonstration of tasting boogers to save the universe on the PA system.

Dr Cherry BEE was furious about everyone's reaction and used telepathy to talk to everyone's mind, "The whole universe is in a state of emergency; stop all this nonsense," and roared tremendously loud, "Back to your position!"

Everyone felt like someone snapped in their face and went back to work quietly. The only person that Dr Cherry BEE could not influence her mind is Lady JJ, because she has an 'absent' mind.

Lady JJ, Luca, LG and Pineking waited until Dr. Cherry BEE settled down, then Monty continued his demonstration. He cleared his snot again and did the first lick on the three booger balls. He paused for a while, and gave it a thought. Then he started to soak each booger ball by licking it over and over again until the booger ball lost its shape and started to turn into slimy snot again.

"Yike! Phew! I cannot stand this anymore!" LG ran away to take a break.

Earth   Pinet   Green Lips

Suddenly, Lady JJ was shocked, "What are those? The tiny bubbles are in all the three booger balls."

Luca shouted, "Get away!" He was about to use the disinfectant that they had developed to disinfect the booger balls.

Monty screamed, "Stop! The true cell of the virus has finally been revealed! I used pure water, H20, to revive the membrane of the Brlingrr Brlingrr virus. My nano sense of my taste buds can identify chemical compounds. And my saliva can decompose any substance into subatomic particles."

Luca was confused, "Why did you revive the virus?"

Monty explained, "SPYS's vaccine and its disinfectant could not neutralize the Brlingrr Brlingrr virus. The Pump Juice that was used in the vaccine and the disinfectant had an incorrect pH level. It only damaged the membrane of the virus and caused it to evolve and adapt to the environment. The true cell of the virus is microscopic, resembling a tiny red crystal. Once it loses its membrane, It mutates to become undetectable and transmit more aggressively by air. The antibodies in the vaccine were engineered to attack the membrane. They have no effect on the inner cell of the virus. This is the reason Earth, Pinet and Green Lips seem to be free of the Brlingrr Brlingrr virus after using the disinfectants; there were no tiny bubbles to be seen. The disinfectant killed its membrane and this left a bigger problem behind. It went airborne and infected all the civilians."

After Monty finished his speech, he felt dizzy and blacked out. He was exhausted and fell into a deep sleep.

Everyone was still very confused, yet worried about Monty. He was sent to the MediBay for a thorough checkup by Dr. Cedric along with five medical droids assisting him. They also worked at the lab next to the MediBay for immediate test results. Pineking, Dr. David and Dr. CG ran some tests on the virus with H2O to confirm Monty's findings were correct.

Then Pineking cried, "We also need to bring down the pH level, otherwise it cannot be used as an adjuvant in the vaccine. It was not acidic enough before, so it only popped the membrane and provoked the virus to mutate and become airborne " Pineking continued, "However, if the pH level of the formula is too low, the Pump Juice cannot cure the symptoms caused by the virus."

Dr. David, Dr. CG and Pineking were facing a huge challenge to readjust the formula again. They tested on many different pH levels of the formula, trying to come up with the right level that will destroy the membrane and cure the symptoms caused by the Brlingrr Brlingrr virus. But, it should not arouse the virus to mutate into another form.

Meanwhile, at the MediBay, Dr Cherry BEE, Lady JJ, LG and Dr. Cedric were still analyzing Monty's body reaction to the virus. Monty laid down on a bed connected with wires to the life support system. It showed that Monty was recovering from the virus during his deep sleep. His own immune system was fighting against the virus with antibodies. Dr. Cedric drew many blood samples and extracted the antibodies from Monty. He sent them to the lab for analysis and waited for the reports. Then he did a scan on Monty's snout and swabbed out some of his snot and saliva for the lab to conduct a report of virus progression. LG read the numbers and the grid on the life support system again and noticed that Monty's health was fully recovered from the Brlingrr Brlingrr virus.

She asked Dr. Cedric, "The system shows that Monty is recovered. Do you think Monty's antibodies could neutralize the Brlingrr Brlingrr virus? This may be the key for the vaccine!"

Dr. Cedric was excited too, yet hesitant, "Yes. Monty's antibodies may be the solution to this pandemic. But, I want to review all the results of the reports before concluding anything. I don't want to make a quick judgment like before. We need to be more careful this time when developing the solution."

After knowing the positive news about Monty, Lady JJ and Dr. Cherry BEE went back to join Luca at the SPYS Control Room to continue supporting the teams on Earth, Pinet, Green Lips and the new SPYS Isolation Center at Unknown.

A medical droid came to Dr. Cedric and LG, and informed them that the reports were completed, all showing negative on the virus. The medical droid projected all the results in holograms surrounding the walls of the MediBay. Dr. Cedric and LG read them carefully and cross-checked the result of each hypothesis. They all concluded that Monty's antibodies could neutralize the core of the Brlingrr Brlingrr virus. Monty was 100% recovered. His immune system produced massive amounts of antibodies while he was in deep sleep.

Dr. Cedric and LG cried in joy. They gathered the team at the lab and announced that the super-antibodies were identified in Monty's immune system. Dr. Cedric asked Dr. David and Dr. CG to prepare for developing a new vaccine with these super-antibodies. However, the adjustment to the pH level of the Pump Juice was not completed yet, and may provoke the Brlingrr Brlingrr virus to mutate again. LG asked Amal to run simulations on different pH levels of the Pump Juice to get the best result to use in the new vaccine and the disinfectant.

While waiting for Amal to generate the result, Dr. Cedric gave a briefing to everyone on each element needed for the vaccine development process. He explained, "We must add the antigen of the virus into the vaccine to trigger an immune response in the host's body. This way, the immune system will battle the virus and memory cells will remember the strategy for defeating it when the real virus comes. Then, we add the adjuvant that boosts up the immune system to battle the antigen. In this case, we need the Pump Juice from Pineking. What is the new pH level that you have adjusted to the formula?"

Pineking replied loudly, "We brought up the pH level to 5. It is still a little bit acidic."

Dr. David added, "It can still damage the membrane and cause the core of the virus to evolve. However, it does not invade the virus as aggressively as before."

Dr. CG suggested, "I think this time, I will not add any glucose in any substances as this will fluctuate the pH level of the Pump Juice too."

LG then informed everyone that Amal found the accurate combination of the pH level in the solution. It ran over millions of combinations on the simulator. She took out a piece of device from her suit and inserted it into the lab system.

Amal projected her findings in holograms and reported, "The results may surprise you. The correct pH level of Pump Juice is 4.5, in order to maximize the effectiveness of the antibody in the new vaccine. At pH level 4.5, the solution can destroy the membrane of the Brlingrr Brlingrr virus and stimulate the new antibody to directly neutralize the core of the virus. The antibodies will also level down the fatality rate and the side effect below 10%. Out of all the combinations, this is the best result for the vaccine. Since a vaccine is a solution with a controlled dosage and measurement, all the results can be calculated and predictable. While making disinfectant, the pH level needs to adjust to 5.5 in the solutions. The pH level can be achieved by diluting it with water. In conclusi–."

Dr. CG interrupted Amal, "Definitely this time, I can add some special substances in the solution to lower down the pH level 5 of the Pump Juice to 4.5." Everyone smiled.

Dr. Cedric was relieved to learn that they had all the answers for the vaccine. He continued to explain the rest of the substances needed for the developing process. He talked about the importance of adding a stabilizer to prevent any unpredictable chemical reactions in the host's body. He also talked about adding preservatives to prevent the vaccine from getting contaminated. And the diluents, like sterile water, were used to dilute the vaccine to the correct dosage. Last to add in the vaccine were surfactants that could keep the vaccine ingredients mixed together evenly to avoid the solution clumping together. After Dr. Cedric gave general information on developing a vaccine, everyone divided into jobs and prepared the substances.

Dr. Cedric called Luca to bring the Vaccine Assembling Line to the lab. He assisted Dr. Cedric and the medical team load the vials into the machine for creating the

Kids Power Academy: Superheroes Assembly

SPYS Star Vaccine Instructions

Type A for solidified subjects:
Impact on subjects

Type B for unsolidified subjects:
Inject into subjects

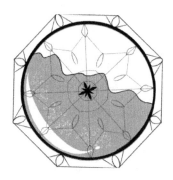

solution. The machine mixed all the substances to the right dosage and filled them in vials. Dr. Cedric reported to Dr. Cherry BEE that the new vaccine was completed and their first subject was IBoy. They had injected the new vaccine in him and were waiting for results.

A few hours later… The new vaccine worked!

IBoy woke up from the coma and gained consciousness. He had recovered from the Blringrr Blringrr virus. No more viruses were detected in his body. Dr. Cherry BEE was glad to hear the good news and asked Luca to open a portal to SPYS Isolation Center on Unknown to deliver the new batch of vaccine to Dr. Crown.

Luca holocalled to the SPYS Control Room, reporting the current condition of the Isolation Center, "Dr. Cherry

163

BEE, the situation here is devastating. Dr. Crown is preparing to vaccinate the subjects. She will give it to the IMT first."

While Luca walked over to IMT, Dr. Cherry saw Myria and Techer on the screen. They looked pale and were lying stiffly on the stretchers.

"They look horrible!" Dr. Cherry BEE mumbled; she paused, then continued, "Luca, I need you to come back to load the disinfectant into the Tubweque. Dr. David and Dr. CG are preparing them. Please send my regards to Dr. Crown. We will triumph over this!" Dr. Cherry BEE sobbed and ended the call.

Luca came back to SPYS Launching Bay from his portal to prepare millions of Tubweques' spray tankers. Dr. David and Dr. CG informed Luca that the new disinfectant was completed, and they were confident that the disinfectant would kill the core of the virus this time, and the solution will convert them into H2O. Luca gave a salute to them and commanded the droids to put the disinfectants into mass production. After the droids filled the Tubweques with disinfectant, Luca programmed the Tubweques to fly over to the infected planets and stars and disinfect them throughout the universe.

Back in the control room, Dr. Crown was on a screen having a holocall with Dr. Cherry BEE. She was delighted,

"IMT is recovering! Their life-support system shows the crystal spikes are disappearing and the viruses are diminishing. I think the vaccine works! Wait, wait!!"

Dr. Crown walked over to Myria. Everyone in the control room saw Myria moving slightly through Dr. Crown's screen.

She yelled, "Myria is awake! She has been in a coma ever since I arrived."

Dr. Crown burst out in tears, and checked on Techer. "He has a regular pulse too. We need more vaccines!"

Dr.Cherry BEE and the whole control room filled with the joy of victory! She responded to Dr. Crown, "We will send more vaccines to you. Keep us posted!"

Dr. Crown nodded in strong agreement and attended to the patients with her team. Dr. Cherry BEE instructed Luca and Dr. Cedric to put the new vaccine in full production and distribute it to all infected planets and stars in the galaxy.

After Dr. Crown reported everyone's health was stable at the Isolation Center, Lady JJ, LG and Luca executed the evacuation plan and started to bring everyone back from Unknown to SPYS Star.

A big celebration was about to start. Monty woke up and entered the control room. He caught up on all the good news just in time

10.
BIG REVEAL

It was a beautiful and healthy day for all the life forms in the universe. All the planets and stars were Brlingrr Brlingrr virus-free. Everyone resumed their own daily routine. Kids Power Academy reopened and students returned to school. The whole campus was filled with good vibes; no hazmat suits were needed. Students could go to parties without staying in their safety bubbles. And now, students had a new place to hang out. LG, Dragon Boy and Pineking refurbished the original secret lab, 'I-CUP Cafe', and renamed it to 'Bling Bling Cafe'. It was Pineking's idea to use this name to symbolize the triumph of their battle over the supervirus, Brlingrr Brlingrr. Since everyone already knew the cafe had a secret lab, LG, Dragon Boy and Pineking opened it for students who are interested in science discovery.

Bling Bling cafe featured two signature drinks, 'Earth COVID-19" and 'Pinet Juice Bugs'. Earth COVID-19 was blue and green and tasted like water and trees. It boosted up superheroes' intelligence to pass all kinds of school-exams.

Pinet Juice Bugs was yellow and green and tasted awfully sour. It was a medicine to help the superheroes detoxing their bodies by pooping out alien bugs. If the students were very hungry and depressed, the cafe had two power snacks that cheered them up in a jiffy. They are 'Green Lips Stone-Lips' and 'The Unknown Disaster!'. Green Lips Stone-Lips was a green lips bun with smelly goo filling. The Unknown Disaster! was a purple explosive cotton candy. The ultimate masterpiece of the cafe was 'Monty's Trace Snot'. It was a cupcake that resembled the shape of Super Detective Monty. It was gray, blue and yellow, and tasted like snot and boogers. It gave a temporary power of nano senses to the superheroes.

On a regular school day, everyone gathered at the Bling Bling Cafe as usual after school. The atmosphere was filled with jokes and laughter! Even the Lipsies visited the cafe more often than before, after the passage reopened at the Wishing Tree. While everyone was happily chit-chatting, Lady JJ's voice rang from the Public Address (P.A.) system:

"Attention students of Kids Power Academy! I am glad to see all of you returning to the campus, happily and healthily. With our greatest gratitude to all the superheroes, S.P.Y.S. Committee and Eyeball facilities... AWrwwweeee" a static noise came through the microphone and everyone could barely hear a voice from behind. "It's SPYS Stars..."

Everybody glanced at each other and groaned. "Here we go again... Same old absent-minded Lady JJ as always..."

We sure are back to normal," a voice alerted everyone at the bar.

Pineking sighed. Everyone laughed out loud.

"Ahem! Excuse me everyone! Correction, with our greatest gratitude to URBAN Committee and SPYS Stars... AWweeeewing" the same static noise rang again."

"Again!!! We don't have all day, Lady JJ. Read from the script!" Everyone was annoyed.

Suddenly, a loud voice came through the P.A. system, "Read!" Everyone noticed that it must've been James.

"OK! OK! You don't have to yell," said Lady JJ. She cleared her voice and continued, "Sorry everyone, we have a technical issue. I will make this really quick:

"With our greatest gratitude to the most respectful super-detective Monty, the super scientists of S.P.Y.S. Committee and SPYS Stars - Science Research Facility: they developed the super vaccine and the disinfectant sprays. All the Brlingrr Brlingrr virus was gone in the universe and everyone recovered from it. We finally triumphed over this supernova pandemic. We regained our health and our normal lives. We have learned to respect each planet's creation and their environments. Although some of us may have lost our loved ones in this battle, we built stronger friendships with our neighbors and became life-long allies. We fought together against all odds, and we can build anything bigger than our universe together... Geeeeee... Geeeee..."

A soft voice from behind appeared again, "Are you finished yet? Everyone is getting impatient! Cut it short!"

Lady JJ continued, "If you feel sick or have any symptoms again, please go directly to our new MediBay at the Central Control tower. This time, we will be prepared, and we will take extra precautions to avoid any disease. That's it for today! Have a wonderful day!" Then she turned off the P.A. system.

"Hooray! Finally! She is done!" shouted everyone at the Bling Bling Cafe.

"Umm... What was Lady JJ's message again?" asked Dragon Boy.

"Eehhh? Who cares! Let's Party!!!!" shouted Pineking.

LG left the cafe and went to check on the Gurion Beast security system. They were withering when LG first saw them on the first day of the academy reopening. LG was so sad and sobbed because she could not continue her project of DNA reengineering of the Gurion Beasts.

She consulted Poison Fang about the condition of the dying Gurion Beasts. He endeavoured to create a new fertilizer and revived them. The Gurion Beasts did not look the same as they were before. In fact, they were more like Gurion babies. They looked like green salad bowls with a big cherry tomato, except this time they were much smaller with a tongue sticking out from the red alarm in the middle. They were noisy; and when they felt bored, they would cry loudly to get attention.

Poison Fang reminded LG to talk to the Gurion babies at least an hour per day, in order for them to grow stronger and faster. They were creatures, not plants, of Guuwen. They were the only Gurion Beasts left in the universe. He also reminded LG to wear a raincoat everytime she talked to the Gurion babies. They would blow raspberries everywhere and even flood themselves with their own saliva. No one wanted to go near them. However, this is the only way that the Gurion babies can get nutritions to grow to maturity.

LG activated her rain poncho, which was integrated in her KPA badge by James. While she approached one of the Gurion babies, she saw a girl next to them. LG was so surprised because all the Gurion babies were very calm.

LG asked, "How did you do that?"

The girl answered, "Huh? Do what?"

LG continued, "How did you calm them down? And you can understand what they say? They usually blow raspberries everywhere and drown themselves in their saliva."

The girl chuckled, "Oh that! You just give them a little bit of this blue sand and they will be friendly to you, and they will talk to your heart. They love this blue sand."

LG was still confused, "How did you know all this?"

The girl explained, "I find the Gurion babies very fascinating. So I went back in time to find their origin. They are from Guuwen."

LG cried, "Woah... Amazing! I am LG, from Earth; nice to meet you! I am doing a DNA reengineering project for increasing the Gurion Beasts reproduction rate."

The girl replied, "I am July, from Math Star, the Crossing Girl. I am a mathematician and an astronomer. I love to travel to different planets and stars to discover new lifeforms. You don't need to do that, they lay eggs and they multiply faster than any bacteria or germs. And this may be a problem."

LG's jaw dropped, "Whaaaaaaaat?"

July invited LG, "Yeah, come with me! I will take you back in time and you will see how they were born."

LG was disappointed, because all the hard work that she spent on her project went down the drain. However, she was overwhelmed with curiosity, so she followed July.

July transformed into Crossing Girl and circled her Crossing Torch in the air to open a Crossing Hole, like a time portal. LG and Crossing Girl travelled back in time to the beginning of Guuwen, 20,000 years ago. The whole planet was covered in blue sand; and it all started with one Gurion Beast. The Gurion Beast layed many eggs rapidly by feeding on the blue sand.

LG was astonished "Woah…"

Crossing Girl nodded, "They lay eggs every minute and multiply exponentially. They are so content by munching on the blue sand. Guuwen will be overwhelmed by Gurion Beasts and gradually devoured in 20,000 years until no more blue sand remains. Gurion Beasts will soon become extinct."

LG was shocked, "OMG! It is happening now, in the present?"

Crossing Girl confirmed LG was correct by nodding her head.

LG gasped in horror, "I need to get some blue sand back to my lab. We have a bigger problem, I cannot let the Gurion Beasts become extinct." Then LG holocalled Luca to prepare a robotic arm. Then Crossing Girl opened a Crossing Hole for Luca to send the robotic arm to 20,000 years ago Guuwen and scooped up a crate of blue sand back to SPYS Star Science Research Facility for further analysis.

LG was so devastated to know that Guuwen was dying. She asked Crossing Girl to open a Crossing Hole to take her to the present Guuwen. Right in front of their eyes, they saw Guuwen was falling apart, covered with millions of withering Gurion Beasts. There was no more blue sand. It was dark, dull and dying.

Tears were running down LG's face as she sobbed, "The scenery is just horrible!"

Crossing Girl was very calm, "I've seen many other planets and stars dying. It was pretty predictable... You just need to pluck in the right elements and numbers, then you will know the lifespan of each planet. That's how I can travel back to the past and the future. It's all about the right calculation. In fact, there is nothing you can do about the planets and stars dying. It's just nature." Crossing Girl hugged LG to comfort her and suggested, "You should continue the DNA reengineering project on the Gurion Beasts. This time, you should focus on how much blue sand they should consume in order to slow down their reproduction rate."

LG agreed. Crossing Girl opened a Crossing Hole and took them back to the campus.

From a far distance, they already heard the noisy Gurion babies blowing raspberries everywhere and causing trouble for everyone. Many students tried to shield themselves away from the Gurion babies' saliva as they passed by. Crossing Girl flew in the air and sprinkled some blue sand in the Gurion babies' mouth. They finally calmed down. LG and Crossing Girl left them in peace for the day.

While LG and Crossing Girl were chatting more about the Gurion Beasts, LG received an urgent holocall from Lady JJ. She informed LG that SPYS Stars Science Research Facility detected a big piece of debris, with undetectable micro life forms on it, was heading towards Pinet. She wanted LG to take a closer look at the debris.

LG smiled at Crossing Girl, "Do you want to go space diving?"

Crossing Girl replied, "Sure! But, are you sure you don't want to use my Crossing Holes?"

LG grinned, "Nah... Let's do some exercise!"

They activated their space suits by touching their KPA badge, which was upgraded by Luca. He removed the hazmat suit from it.

"Are you ready?" asked LG.

"Yup!" replied Crossing Girl, "Should we bring our pets along. My TC looks like a cloud. She is a creature from Planet SKY. She loves to go space diving!"

LG replied, "Oh yeah! I should bring along Starlight too, an animal from planet Fur, which looks like a wolf."

Crossing Girl and LG fetched their pets. *Zooooooooooooom!* They all went space diving in the galaxy.

They had tremendous fun doing their solo stunts and totally forgot their mission. LG blasted out electric streaks in space and she zoomed through them. She repeated the same stunt over and over again. Crossing Girl did a ballet dance in fast motion, like a time-laspe. TC and Starlight were always their owners' loyal fans. Their eyes gazed at their owners' every move.

However, their hearts told them something else, "These girls are unbelievably ridiculously hilarious. They totally forgot what they needed to do."

Suddenly this happened...

"Ouch! What? What hit me?" LG shrieked and rubbed her head.

Crossing Girl shouted at LG, "Are you okay?"

Both of them were surrounded by millions, billions, trillions of space debris.

"OMG! What is all this waste doing here? We need to find the debris heading towards Pinet. It is an urgent matter!" LG was anxious and knew she made a mistake.

Crossing Girl suggested, "Let's use the Crossing Hole to take everyone near Pinet first, we already wasted so much time." Crossing Girl opened a portal and they saw a big debris falling towards Pinet.

"GO!!" LG charged at the big chunk of debris. She slung out her thudrangs to lasso it. She tried to pull it to a complete stop, but it was too heavy. Crossing Girl, Starlight and TC went behind LG and pulled the thudrangs until the hunk came to a halt. They observed the piece of debris closely. It looked like a fallen part of a spacecraft from Earth. It had some black substance on it similar to the dead corpses of the Knowers, some green slime and pinon crumbs. Starlight kept on howling because of the awful smell. Even Crossing Girl and LG could smell it through their space suits.

Crossing Girl complained, "It is awful with all this waste in space! When does this happen?"

"I found some bubbles!" cried a soft and tiny voice.

"Huh? Who was that?" asked LG.

Crossing Girl said, "That was TC, my cloud."

Everyone went to the spot and shouted together, "Brlingrr Brlingrr virus!" They exchanged looks and panicked.

LG immediately holocalled Lady JJ, "Lady JJ! We stopped the debris from falling to Pinet! We found some tiny bubbles on the debris. Here, I will show them to you through my camera. Do you think that they are Brlingrr Brlingrr virus? We don't want to get too close because we don't have the hazmat suit on. Can you do an analysis on the bubbles?"

Lady JJ was speechless and spaced out. She was confused because the universe was supposed to be free from the virus.

LG continued, "And please look at this, we are surrounded by millions and billions of waste in space. It is awfully smelly here! Hello! Hello! Lady JJ, are you there?"

Lady JJ snapped back in consciousness, "Yep, I am here! Right, let me call Luca to do an analysis on the debris."

In a few seconds, Luca in a hazmat suit opened a portal and used a giant lobster clasp to pull the piece of debris to SPYS Stars Science Research facility. Luca informed LG and Crossing Girl that the analysis will come out in three minutes. LG and Crossing Girl checked on some of the waste in space and found out all of them had tiny bubbles. They found that the situation was very disturbing.

Lady JJ called them again and confirmed the tiny bubbles were Brlingrr Brlingrr virus. LG reported that they randomly checked on the waste in space and they all carried the tiny bubbles. Lady JJ told LG, Crossing Girl, TC and Starlight to stay put, she will order Luca to send two thousand Tubweques, with disinfectant tanks, to them. Lady JJ asked LG to gather the superheroes to disinfect all the waste in the galaxy. Then, she ended the call.

LG asked Starlight to flash her horn, calling for all the superheroes nearby to come together. In a split of a second, thousands of them appeared. They greeted each other and were surprised to see all this space pollution. While LG explained everything, Luca opened a portal and delivered two thousand Tubweques to them. Once the superheroes were inside, the Tubweque disinfected them and protected them from the virus. Then, all the superheroes started to spray the disinfectants on the waste, to make sure there was no more virus left in the galaxy. The disinfectant spray converts the virus into clean mineral water. Crossing Girl asked TC to absorb all the clean mineral water and store it for supplying developing planets and stars. Everybody was happy to be rid of all the virus and called it a day, except for LG.

LG and Starlight flew back to the Control Room of Kids Power Academy and saw Lady JJ having multiple conferences with different leaders of different planets and stars regarding space pollution. She summoned an Universal Emergency Conference (UEC) about space pollution at SPYS Stars Science Research facility tomorrow. The call ended.

LG approached Lady JJ, "What is all this?"

Lady JJ was exhausted, "Let's go to SPYS Stars. Luca will explain everything to us there. Space pollution is a serious issue."

Lady JJ and LG flew on Lady JJ's private jet and arrived at SPYS Star's launching bay.

Dr. Cherry BEE was informed about their arrival and arranged for someone to lead them to the Space Operation Room. LG was shocked to see everyone was so busy, running around in the facility, like they were preparing for a war. Lady JJ was quiet the whole time with a blunt face. LG had never seen her like this before. Once they entered the room, there were over twenty scientists sitting there, waiting for them. It was more like an auditorium than a regular meeting room. There were many projectors installed around the room and the walls were green. It was furnished like a Virtual Reality (VR) room. There was no meeting table, just rows of seats. and a podium. LG was amazed by the technology of this Space Operation Room.

Dr. Cherry BEE approached them with a serious look, "Please have a seat. The meeting is about to start." They all settled down and Dr.Cherry BEE spoke again, "Luca, please proceed."

Luca came to the podium and showed a hologram of the piece of space debris to everyone. It was the debris falling to Pinet and was stopped by LG earlier today. Then it was taken to SPYS Stars. Luca started to explain, "This is the debris that was found with the bubbles, earlier this morning. We ran some tests on the bubbles and analyzed the data. The results were affirmative. They are the Brlingrr Brlingrr virus."

Everyone gasped and murmured.

Luca showed another hologram and continued, "This is the picture, given by Lady JJ, of our space right now. Our galaxy is polluted by all kinds of waste from different planets. LG and thousands of other superheroes were there late this afternoon to disinfect all the waste. Perhaps, LG could tell us more about what she saw out there."

LG went to the podium and described the scenario of the space pollution, "It was horribly massive in size. There were Knowers' corpses everywhere, toxic slime from Green Lips, rotten pinon sludge from Pinet, broken space crafts and other equipment from Earth, decaying fur from Furball... And a whole lot more. They decompose and then bond together to make bigger debris. They will also emit some sort of heat that releases extremely smelly odors."

Luca stepped in while LG returned to her seat. He then showed another hologram, "Yes, this is the most terrifying part. The space pollution created the supervirus, Brlingrr Brlingrr, by vertex radiation. This vertex radiation was formed when those wastes bonded together."

All the scientists muttered with each other about this radiation.

Luca asked everyone to quiet down, "Now that we know the problem, I need everyone to come up with a solution. We need to build a machine or a station to collect all the waste and convert the vertex radiation into energy. This is the only way to save our universe. We need a construction plan by tomorrow to present it to all the leaders of the universe. Everyone please study the space debris at the lab and run necessary tests on it."

Then Dr. Cherry BEE announced, "The Universal Emergency Conference will be held tomorrow morning at 10:00, here at the Space Operation Room. Let's get to work. We have loads to do tonight. Meeting adjourned!"

Lady JJ and LG spent a night at SPYS Star Science Research facility to work together with the scientists and Dr. Cherry BEE.

Next morning, all the leaders of all planets and stars arrived on time for the Universal Emergency Conference about space pollution. They took seats at the Space Operation Room and waited for Lady JJ to start the conference. Lady JJ came to the podium and explained the critical condition of space pollution in the universe. The universe cannot bear the mass of the waste being tossed out of each planet and star any longer. She explained that if space pollution doesn't stop, another Supernova Pandemic will happen soon.

Lady JJ spoke, "Yesterday, LG and thousands of other superheroes came together and disinfected all the waste in space, because the Brlingrr Brlingrr virus appeared again. We need to get rid of all the waste in space right now to clear the universe. Then, we need to do waste management. I'll let Dr. Cherry BEE and Luca explain the solution to us." Lady JJ stepped down back to her seat and gave the floor to Dr. Cherry BEE and Luca.

Dr. Cherry BEE presented the solution, a SPYS Waste Converter Station (SPYS WCS), to the leaders. It was designed by the scientists of SPYS Star Science Research facility. She suggested each planet build their own SPYS

WCS. For the dwarf planets and stars, SPYS Star will set up one million SPYS Central Waste Management Stations (SPYS CWMS) for them.

Dr. Cherry BEE expressed in delight, "All those stations not only manage waste for the planet, but it can convert them into energy. I'll let Luca explain more."

Dr. Cherry BEE was dismissed and Luca came to the podium. First he showed a few holograms of the current condition of space pollution to let the leaders have a better understanding of the critical situation in the universe. Then he showed another hologram about captive debris from yesterday. It showed green slime, Knower's corpses, Earth's broken spaceship debris, rotten pinon juice and much more. Above all that were bubbles, tons of them, identified as Brlingrr Brlingrr virus.

Then Luca showed the third hologram and explained, "This is how vertex radiation formed: when the waste bonded together, they emitted unknown energy which transmitted vertex radiation. This hologram shows you the waste bonding and emitting vertex radiation. Our scientists ran some test on it and discovered the vertex radiation is the catalyst for the microorganism to grow into a Brlingrr Brlingrr virus."

Luca continued to explain the process of converting vertex radiation into energy before it turns into Brlingrr Brlingrr virus. They invented a converter. Luca handed out the construction plan of the converter to each leader and demonstrated on a hologram.

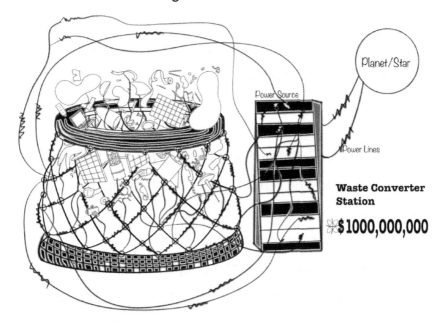

"This SPYS Waste Converter Station or SPYS WCS was designed and patented by SPYS Star Science Research Facility. We can dispose our waste through this pipe." He pointed to the pipe attached to the converter. "Then the converter will break down the waste into subatomic particles and the vertex radiation will be converted to energy. In the end, the energy will be transmitted through power lines and supply the planet. The

SPYS Central Waste Management Station will produce energy and store it in rechargeable batteries. Dwarf planets can collect the batteries back to their planets after they dispose their waste."

Next, Luca showed a cost table on the screen, "Here is the reality, the cost of this converter is..." Luca paused for dramatic effect. All the leaders gasped in fear. "It costs $100,000,000 Universal Dollars per SPYS WCS. Or you can help SPYS Star to build the one million SPYS CWMS for the dwarf planets."

There was a moment of silence, then all the leaders began muttering and mumbling and murmuring, until they came to a conclusion. They agreed to build the one million SPYS CWMS for the dwarf planets.

Lady JJ took out a Galaxy Agreement for all the leaders to sign. Each one agreed to take their responsibility of reducing waste and achieving a clean universe. Kids Power Academy will provide waste management training on the 3Rs: Reuse, Reduce and Recycle to all the universal civilians.

"The beneficial effects of applying the 3Rs :
- Prevents pollution caused by reducing the need to harvest new raw materials
- Saves energy

- Reduces greenhouse gas emissions that contribute to global climate change
- Helps sustain the environment for future generations
- Saves money
- Reduces the amount of waste that will need to be recycled or sent to landfills and incinerators
- Allows products to be used to their fullest extent"

Website: Climate Change The New Economy (CCTNE)

Issued date of article: June 15, 2018

A month later, the universe was clean and cleared. Universal civilians went space diving more often and did more out-space exercises. Lady JJ and Dr. Cherry BEE were happy to see the whole universe was healthy.

LG said, "The space is galactically beautiful! We should do our ultimate best to protect it."

And they all enjoyed space diving.

11.
SUPERHEROES'
PROFILES

Scan the QR codes to see the original portraits of each Superhero or Superscientist, and read their writer's messages.

Don't forget to **Like & Follow** to get your badge!

LG, The Lightning Girl
In Ch 1, 2, 6, 7, 8, 9&10

Created & written by
**Alia Spring Kong, 10
Lead Author, Editor &
Illustrator of** *Supernova
Pandemic*

Spring is from Earth and a
senior student of Kids Power
Academy. She has a purple
ponytail and wears a shoulder
length turquoise shirt, black
shorts and sneakers. She
studies micro and
macroscopic anatomy and
experiments on chemical compounds. Spring is a
compassionate and gracious girl, and always shows
empathy towards others. When Spring transforms into LG,
she puts her fists above her head and releases her grasps.
Her hair flows in the air and resembles buns pinned with
Thudrangs, Lightning Bolt hair clips.

LG twirls and waves her hands above her head to
make two big 'S' curves crossing each other. A tiara will
appear on her head with a pair of smart glasses. She has a
black bulletproof shirt with a lightning bolt sign in the middle,
a suit integrated with an artificial intelligence system. LG can

command it for any operation using her glasses. She wears white pants with orange and gold jagged ribbons. And she flies with her purple rocket boots. She is the youngest advisor of the S.P.Y.S. Committee at SPYS Stars.

LG's lightning power has kinetic energy, which includes thermal energy and electrical energy ①. She can control them at different voltage levels. LG's powers have accelerated 10 times stronger than before. A normal lightning bolt contains 300 million ② volts of energy. LG's

Spacerike bolts contain 3 billion volts of electricity! LG's Splatongs are electric bombs with hot metal beads and a cloud on top. When it comes into impact, it will crack open and beads roll everywhere. The friction created by the beads rubbing against each other will turn into thermal energy. The positive charged particles rise to the top of the cloud and the negative charged particles sink down to the bottom of the cloud. Once they grow big enough, lightning will shoot out③. All this happens within less than a second.

LG's Thudrangs are like a skipping rope. It is the upgraded version of the lasso. LG tamed it by 'tangling' it in her hair. Thudrang is good to use for catching targets. It is also a 50,000 volts taser ④. LG communicates with Thudrangs through her sweat.

LG can speak multiple universal languages with different civilians in the galaxy. Those languages have many strokes that resemble like Chinese-characters. LG gathers intels from different planets as a polyglot. LG can space dive spinning into a tornado for defense by collecting hot and cold air.

Starlight is a wolf from Planet Fur. She has white fur and sapphire eyes. She also has a pair of aqua wings and a yellow horn on her head. When she sings, her fur glows yellow. Her voice can boost up her team's energy level. Her glowing yellow fur  will give the enemy sore eyes and put them to sleep. LG will play the Riol, like a violin, to amplify Starlight's singing. When Starlight spots trouble, she will flash her horn. The heroes nearby will come for the rescue.

1.'Everything you need to know to ace Science' Unit 4: Energy - Pg. 129 - 137
2. National Weather Service How powerful is lightning? July 9, 2021
   https://www.weather.gov/safety/lightning-power
3.Planet Science - Article: What causes lightning? July 9, 2021
   http://www.planet-science.com/categories/over-11s/natural-world/2012/06/what-causes-lightning.aspx
4.U.S Energy Information Administration (FIA), Article: What is Energy?
   June 18, 2020 https://www.eia.gov/energyexplained/what-is-energy

Dr. Crown
In Ch 1, 6&7

Created by
Mira Chen, 5
Written by her mom,
Mavis Chao

Dr. Crown is an artificially enhanced human girl, and she is the smartest kid on Earth. At the age of 8, she had already finished school and achieved 11 postgraduate degrees, including PhDs in Chinese, English, French, German, Korean, and Mathematics. She also has a degree of Doctor of Medicine. She is now 9 years old. Dr. Crown has beautiful long black hair. She always wears a golden crown. Unlike most doctors who wear lab coats, Dr. Crown likes to wear pink pajamas with orange checkers. Staying comfortable helps her think and work better.

Dr. Crown created many inventions, like her crown. She designed many vertical lines across the crown with crystal dots sitting on top of them. The lines are portal doors. The crystal dots on the crown can beam out shrink rays to shrink Dr. Crown and her companion cat, Fuzzy, small enough to pass through the portal doors on the crown. Once Dr. Crown and Fuzzy reach their destination, the crystal dots will beam Dr. Crown and Fuzzy back to their original size. Dr. Crown keeps this as a secret to keep the crown safe.

Dr. Crown creates weapons for many superheroes who can pass Fuzzy's test to prove themselves to have a good heart. Fuzzy's super power allows her to see into people's hearts.. Dr. Crown created many invisible weapons for Invisible Boy.

Fuzzy is an artificially enhanced cat and she is Dr. Crown's companion. She is soft like cotton candy and her fur is pink. Fuzzy has powerful strength. She is Dr. Crown's bodyguard. Her special attack-move is called SqueezyHug. Fuzzy attacks her enemies by hugging and squeezing them. The enemies will be tied up into a furball and cannot get out until they sincerely promise that they will not do bad things anymore. Fuzzy has super instincts, so she can tell whether a promise is true or not.

A-Girl
In Ch 1, 4&8

Created & written by
Alina Chao, 12
Main Contributor to Ch 4

Claire is a 12-years-old scientist of SPYS Star Science Facility. She has a brown ponytail and her daily outfit is a rosy- purple T-shirt with a pair of jeans and shiny blue sneakers. She excels in math and can perform complicated calculations in just one snap. She is an energetic girl. And she is very determined to go after her belief.

Claire always wears a silver necklace with an 'A'charm. When Claire touches it, she will transform into A-Girl in a flash. Her hair is tied up into a bun with a silver string. She wears a cream-colored T-shirt inside and a light purple cardigan The cardigan was technologically enhanced and is fireproof. She also wears a pair of denim jeans with cartoon patterns.

Claire has a weapon to launch super sticky bombs to stick the enemies to the ground. She is a biologist and makes potion bombs. She has a small collection of potions made from different elements. Those are for emergency uses.

Cottonbell is a fluffy puppy, Claire's best friend. Claire found her in an animal shelter while expediting her science journey in Europe. Cottonbell has snow white fur and jade green eyes. Her fur is not just soft but can help her fly because it has "Fly powders". It can make technologically enhanced tools out of cotton with only a wave of her paws. Cottonbell rides on her rocket-fast motorbike to get anywhere.

Ms. D
In Ch 2

Created & written by
Sherise Chan, 14
Contributor to Ch 2

Ms Dominique is the captain of Team Resilience, the medical team of S.P.Y.S. Committee. She is a polyglot and specializes in medical science. She is realistic and straight-forward. She has good judgment to ensure there are no mistakes made. She wears a blouse and a long skirt with a braid. She has excellent vision, yet she still enjoys wearing glasses occasionally as she thinks the accessory complements her appearance.

When she is in superhero mode, her hair magically becomes short. Her outfit changes to an orange t-shirt with overalls and boots. They are technologically enhanced which lets her move ten times faster than the ordinary she.

198

Ms Dominique creates innovative weapons and medical equipment. She can heal people with energy medicine through her empathic, astral, mental and spiritual energy. She has an alarm that rings in her head when there's trouble nearby. She uses telepathy to read minds and transmit thoughts to them. This can help her track the cause of any problem. Her extraordinary vision and medical skill helps her endeavor many solutions.

Ms Dominique is Team R's leader and a role model. Her medical team includes Iris,the Cat Lady and Snowball. Each of them are specialized in different science fields. They have unique superpowers. Together, they form a special task force and they are stronger than ever to battle against any virus!

Cat Lady
In Ch 2

Created & written by
**Candy Zhang, 10
Contributor to Ch 2**

Iris is a 25 years old biologist from a C-planet. She is a smart, kind and courageous lady. She is always helpful. She loves music, literature, and fine arts. She never sees anything clearly because she is near-sighted. She does not wear any glasses because they will cover her big round charming eyes. She likes her short brown hair. Her favourite outfit is a light pink polka-dot dress and a pair of baby-blue tall boots.

Iris was turned into Cat Lady because she was bitten by a cat-like creature in an experiment. She then had a cat face, a tail and was covered with short brown fur all over her body. She dresses in a short blue dress and a belt with "CL" written on it. She flies with her cape and does power jumps with her tall boots.

She has night vision like a cat when she blinks her eyes three times. Her eyes would glow like flashlights to help her find targets at night. And She can see microscopic things like bacteria and viruses. She has rocket-speed and can run as fast as a leopard. She can do power jumps, and can jump six meters high. She has a sensitive nose, and can smell danger nearby. Her weakness is water. If she touches water, she will lose all her super powers and transform back into Iris. And her fish hairpin will turn to red when she is weak. After she has enough dried fish, the hairpin will turn yellow again, and she can turn back to Cat Lady.

Iris is a member of Team R, responsible for scanning microscopic organisms in their surroundings. Each member wears a SPYS batch to activate their own hazmat suit in the mission to prevent any contact of the virus. And it acts as a communicator with any life forms during interaction.

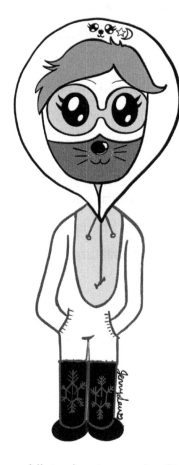

Snowball In Ch 2

Created & written by
Vivian Chu, 8
Contributor to Ch 2 & 4

Snowball is a 9 years old girl. She has long hair. She wears a magenta eye mask and a purple face mask. And she puts on a white seal hat. She wears a jumpsuit and a pair of snowflake boots. Snowball is a brave and kind girl. She is reliable. She helps animals who are in danger. She loves singing songs and listening to music. She likes strawberry ice cream. She is afraid of small bugs. She would jump up and run away if they were targeting her.

Her primary power is farting ice poop. She has a Snow rope for catching bad guys. It can turn them to snow. Her Ice Breath can freeze the enemies. The Snow TNT can blow up the villains into snowflakes. It can also shoot out pink soap bubbles. When the enemy comes into contact with the bubble, the enemy will be trapped inside those unbreakable bubbles. The bubbles will absorb all the energy from the bad guys and they will become weak. Her only weakness is bugs. She will lose her mind and cause a disaster.

Silver is a seal and it is Snowball's pet. They are the best partners to fight against all odds. Silver has snow-white fluffy fur, and sometimes is very naughty. She likes to prank others. Her strongest power is called Cake TNT. Silver's enemies will explode into cakes when she uses Cake TNT. Her fur will turn into a rainbow when she is mad. Her rainbow fur will make explosions and blow up everything around her. The explosion will disappear after she has calmed down.

PineKing
In Ch 3, 4,8&9

Created & written by
**Ryder Chow, 7
Contributing Author
of Ch 3 & 4, and
Artist**

Ryan is from PINET. He grew up and is now 8 years old. Ryan wears a blue t-shirt with a red car logo in the center, with straight black hair on the side. Ryan transforms to Pineking when he senses danger. He is the king of planet "PINET" and lives in Pinecastle. His weight is 100 kilograms, and 2 meters in height, so he looks gigantic. His eyes are green and skin is peach. He wears a shirt with a pineapple logo in the center and a green cape at the back. He loves flying around the universe and loves singing and socializing with his friends. He is smart, curious and kind, so he likes to help others as well.

Pineking's primary power is a healing and damaging potion. The healing potion heals people when pineking throws it on the ground in a 1 by 1 meter radius for 10 seconds. The potion immediately forms a tub that has been filled up with invisible healing liquid. The damaging potion creates the same thing, except it drowns enemies in poison.

His secondary power is he can make pineapple walls to form a maze at the exact location. He traps the enemies inside the maze so Pineking will have more time to throw the damaging potion to defeat the enemies. If the enemy cannot solve the maze in time, then the maze will shrink and constrict the enemy. He also has pineapple mines that will instantly become invisible, only Pineking and other buddies can see them. So when the enemies step on the mines or go near them, the mines will  explode. He uses his powers to fight enemies and protect his planet. Because Pineking's body is full of water, he gets weakened while he stays under the sun for over 7 hours. In order to recharge, he needs to stay in water for one minute to absorb the water that he lost back.

Pineking has a very special belt that has the potions and a time machine. The time machine can help him travel to the past, future and present. It can also pause time, fast forward and rewind time to make it back to normal, all while keeping the user normal speed. He can also summon a microphone from the sky and sing "Pineapple sugar high, Pineapple sugar high" so loud that the sound waves blast people away.

Pineking has a pet dragon named Gragoo. His body is oval shape, and color is black with small white stars. He has wings outlined with black and filled with navy colour for the inside of the wings. His tail is long and is ruffled at the

end. He also wears a ginormous crown, so it is covering his eyes. He listens to the enemy's plans and tells Pineking so that he can tell his buddies about their enemy's defeat plan. Gragoo flies quietly and camouflages with his surroundings.

Gragoo loves playing with his dragon friends about a game called "burn the target". In this game,there is a moving target, they will use ice breath to freeze the target, and then use fire breath to burn him/her down.

Smiling
In Ch 3

Created & written by
Wong Wan Pui, 9

Smiling is a 10 years old girl. She is from Planet Color. Everything is colorful and sparkling . She loves eating pineapples...She is thin and short. She has long silvery hair and blue eyes. She wears a pair of thick-rimmed glasses. Smiling often carries a big smile on her face. Smiling is cheerful, helpful, and nice. She likes drawing and playing the piano. She wears a colorful dress with some pineapple pattern. If she is in a bad mood, her colorful dress will turn black, brown or grey.

Smiling's grandma gave her a magic pastel book. When she opens the pastel book, she will become a superhero. Her primary power is whatever she drew on the pastel book will become true. When people are in danger, Smiling will draw what the people need and save them. Howevershe could not draw well. She could draw a leopard without a leg, which made the leopard unable to run. So she practises drawing very hard every day. Now she draws very well. Smiling's secondary power is that she can make people or herself invisible. When she points to the person who needs to be invisible and yells, "Get invisible". Then, that person will be invisible for 30 minutes.

Smiling has a piano that it can enlarge and shrink. It can melt people's hearts. Smiling's thick-rimmed glasses can make her see the enemy ambushing from behind.

Smiling has a pet rabbit called Angela. She lives in Smiling's hair. Her body is white and her eyes are red. Her eyes have infrared sensors which can quickly spot the enemy.

Little Porter In Ch 3

Created & written by
Jason Chan, 8

Little Porter is an eight years old superhero. He is a sweet boy and a third grade student. When he was a little kid, he always wanted to be a superhero because he wanted to protect this beautiful world. His favorite sport is basketball and his favourite subject is math. He wears a blue shirt with a lightning logo in the center and a red cape. He is only 1.3 meter tall before turning into a superhero, but he will become 2 meters tall when he transforms into a potter fire superhero.

One day, Little Porter saw a strange-looking box in a basketball court. He opened it and suddenly a superhero showed up and told him that " You, Little Porter, are a super-capable child. Therefore, you shall save people who are in fires. You can use the two hours limited fire prevention function to fly into the fire and save everyone. Otherwise the fire prevention function will turn off and you will be injured. This function will only last 2 hours and you need to recharge another hour in order to use this function again" Since then, Little Potter became a brave fire fighting superhero.

Little Porter can also fly with his red rocket shoes. He loves flying around to see if anyone is in danger because of the fire trap.

Little Porter has a best friend called Nono. It is his favorite pet. Nono is yellow with brown dots in the body. It wears red rocket boots to match with the Little Porter too. It uses his nose to sense fire and tells little porter where it is on fire, so that the Little Porter can fly there immediately to put out the fire and rescue others.

Naky
In Ch 3

Created by **Sharon Tang, 11**
Written by Ryder Chow, 7

Kate is a 10 years old girl. She is an introvert. She is shy and doesn't make friends easily. Whenever she feels lonely, she will transform into the superhero "Naky". Naky is a gentle, brave, and intelligent superhero, and she is good at medical science.

She has curly blond hair and big watery black eyes. She wears a green jade necklace, a white scarf, and a pink shirt. Naky has x-ray eyes that can zoom in to see things clearly even if they are very tiny. She also has another medical skill: she can summon a mini flying robot that can be placed on the ground and fly into an injured or virus infected person's body to cure them. When she loses her necklace, she will lose her power.

Naky has a mini bunny pet named "Reta". It looks like an iceberg. Reta can make ice packs, ice stretchers, and also a slippery ice ramp. If a patient cannot move, the patient can slide on the ramp to get from one place to another place.

Blob Man
In Ch 4

Created & written by
Daniel Zhu, 8

Paul is an 8 years old boy who likes to watch his brother doing science experiments. He also likes to discover ancient fossils and read books, because he always finds them mysterious and interesting. Paul was transformed into a 'blob' by accidentally drinking one of his brother's potions. Now he is known as Blob Man. He has orange hair and is covered in red blobs which look like melting jelly. He wears a one piece suit with an "B" symbol in the middle. His weaknesses are potatoes and water. He will faint when he touches potatoes. And water will turn him into sticky glue which makes him difficult to move. Fortunately, he can regain consciousness by eating seaweed.

Blob man has the ability to fly and breathe in space without any devices. He can also fit through tiny holes, about 2 millimeters wide. And he can turn almost into anything, such as keys, balls, trees…etc. He is also good at aiming that he has never missed a target.

Blob man has a pet snake named Diablo. He has flame-red scales and burnt-brown eyes. Diablo's power is Pyrokinesis, he can control any flame from anywhere within 100 kilometers away to start wildfires. Blob man found him in the desert of a planet during a sandstorm. The snake was lost so he took her back to his home.

Minacko
In Ch 4

Created by **Abbygail Liu, 7**
Written by Alia Kong, 11
Illustrated by Vicky Ding, 12

Minacko is 9 years old and an energetic girl. She is very interested in reading mysterious stories with her grandma. . Minacko is from Earth, but now lives in a place called the Old Oak with her siblings, Sika, Mel and Dudu. They have superpowers like mind reading power, super strength and micro-vision. Minacko did not discover her powers until she was a teenager. Her siblings taught her to stabilize her power. She has silky orange hair with a half ponytail. And she wears a long white dress with two bows, a big one at the back and a small one on the chest. She also wears a pair of black leather shoes.

Her power is animus. She can enchant any object or weather in any state of matter. Once she throws her headband into the whirling wind, she can funnel the tornadoes into a tiny worm. She also uses her energy medicine to heal injured people.

Her brother, Dudu, likes to discover new powers with Minacko. Dudu is timid, so Minacko always defends him from threats. They often like to go on a vacation with their family and visit their grandma and listen to her new discovery.

Wina
In Ch 5&6

Created & written by
Vicky Ding, 12
Contributing Author of Ch 5,
and Illustrator

Wina is a girl from
Earth. She likes mysterious
things and sometimes she can
sense things that others
cannot. She wears a white T-
shirt, a black shorts and a pair
of socks.

One day, she saw some
scientists from SPYS Star and
followed them for their journey. Then she agreed to join an
experiment. So scientists used special powders to combine
Wina with a wolf together and put her in some green liquids.
After that, Wina cannot talk well but her voice is as loud as a
wolf. People can hear her voice even a kilometer away. She
has sharp fangs and super hearing like a wolf.

Her body can change into different forms——human ,
werewolf, and wolf. She will change form according to the
environment. Wina can howl like a wolf and the sound wave

can toss enemies away. The special powder allows her to monitor things that others cannot see. Wina is an Alpha wolf, and she can summon wolves. The wolf pack has the same power as Wina. Wina can multiply herself.

Wina's best friend is the wolf who did the transformation with her. Wina has a place for the wolf in her mind that she can communicate with him. And Wina will never feel lonely. They work well together. Sometimes they quarrel,but their friendship is bigger.

Majestic Girl
In Ch 5, 6&9

Created & written by
Chloe Mo, 10
Illustrated by
Vicky Ding, 12

Myria was born in a magical realm that is unknown to all existence. Her parents died in a tragic accident when she was one year old. Two strangers adopted her and gave her their powers. She is very mischievous and loves to prank people. But she is always kind and she loves animals. She wears a colorful t-shirt and long grey baggy pants.

When Myria turns into a superhero, she becomes the majestic girl. Her appearance does not change but her skills and power have advanced her. Myria's eyes twinkle and sparkle to turn bigger in size when she fights the villains.

Myria floats in the air with her boots, without any need of a magical tool. Her boots can blast a strong surge of energy to attack the villains. Myria's greatest power is to create illusions. These fake images can fool the villains for 3 minutes or longer. She can only use it twice a day.

Mryia has a very good friend named Perille. Perille is a very loyal phoenix and serves only to Myria. Perille can go into fires because she is fireproof. She is like the descendant of a blaze, but combined with a bird. Perille is very hard working and loves new ideas, but she can be very ignorant and selfish sometimes.

Invisible Boy
In Ch 5, 6&9

Created & written by
Marcus Chen, 8
Contributor to Ch 3 & 5
Illustrated by Vicky Ding, 12

Invisible Boy (also known as "I-Boy") is a mysterious boy who can turn invisible. He was born on a volcanic planet named Volth, and he is 14 years old.

Even though I-Boy is young, he is an expert car racer with a specially granted driver's license. He achieved Class S, which stands for "Super" and Top "Secret". I-Boy named his cool car Invismoblie, which can turn invisible and can fly. Once it is invisible in the air , no one can find him. I-Boy also owns a cool collection of weapons that were created by Dr. Crown. They can only be seen and used by him; therefore, his weapons can never be stolen.

Invisible Boy has a little furry dog named Boston that protects him. Boston can create an invincible shield. This shield is so powerful that once it was activated, even an atomic bomb cannot break it. Boston earns a nickname of the Invincible Shield Dog. The only drawback of Boston's ability is that he can only use the shield three times a day. The shield power will regenerate over time. Boston can also fight very well and won a gold medal in a fighting game. Boston can turn invisible on I-Boy's command.

Invisible Boy and Boston are inseparable. Boston always rides along with I-Boy on Invisimobile. He sits behind I-Boy and his seat compartment can detach from the main body and turn into another small invisible car.

Techer
In Ch 5, 6&9

Created & written by
Cyrus Chan, 9
Assisted by Vicky Ding, 12

Techer or Tech is a 16-years-old boy from an alternate universe. He likes solving mysteries and sometimes can fix or make gadgets for others. He wears a black suit and black shoes with neon blue stripes. He is a detail-oriented boy.

He won first place in a gadget-making competition. He made an artificially enhanced laser gun, while other competitors made only normal guns. He is the best gizmo inventor. Techer can hear things others can't because of his power suit. He can move at supersonic speed. He has superhuman strength. He can teleport his gadgets, vehicles, and aircraft. He can fly with his jetpack. He has laser guns like laser pistol, laser cannon, laser sniper, laser ac-58 and laser ray. He can make force shields to protect himself and others.

Techer's assistant is a bot that he made when he was 9 years old. He named it Bop. Bop has been upgraded now. Techer discusses battle strategies with Bop when they are fighting with enemies. They can do anything together.

Dr. Cedric
In Ch 6&9

Created & written by
Catherine Chao, 11
Main Contributor to
Ch 6

Doctor Cedric is a 11 years old boy whose Intelligence Quotient (IQ) is 300. He is the smartest scientist on Earth. He broke many records in the Science Community such as the youngest winner of the Nobel Prize in Chemistry. He and his brother Charlie built a Secret Underground Lab together. It is used as a portal to SPYS Star, the Science Research Facility. He dresses in a lab coat with his name on it and the long black pants. He also wears a blue and white-stripes scarf around his neck. He is an adventurous boy who likes to explore new places.

Doctor Cedric can read minds so he can know what others were thinking about. He uses his 'sharp' eyesight and strong hearing power to locate troubles. He can make weather bubbles and stir up any weather conditions for research purposes. He can also become invisible, and uses his telekinesis power to move things around.

Dr. Cedric has a giant snow phoenix named Snowy. He is Dr. Cedric's best friend. Snowy is his bodyguard, transportation and helper. It has snow white feathers with icy blue eyes and a long white tail. It's special move is called Blinding Flash. When they are in danger, Snowy will start glowing and the light will blind the enemies. Before the enemies could open their eyes, he and Doctor Cedric would disappear. Snowy's tears also have healing powers that Cedric usually collected for making healing potions.

Miss GG
In Ch 6

Created & written by
Li Zhi Qing, 11
Assisted by Alia Kong, 10
Illustrated by Vicky Ding, 12

Lily is a kind and positive girl. She has long black hair and a pair of soulful eyes. Her daily outfit is a pink shirt and a blue tutu, along with a pair of sneakers. When Lily transforms into Miss GG, her hair is tied up into a flowing ponytail. She also has a pair of transparent butterfly wings along with a lace up burgundy dress and a pair of bouncing, rocket boots.

Miss GG has Pyrokinesis. She can shoot out fireballs at any degree with her hands and control any flame from anywhere. She has a magical chain that spouts water, which can wipe out moraine.. She also carries two fire guns on her arm. It can help to shoot fire rocks, like meteors, at light speed to the enemies.

Miss GG has a pet cat named Dash. When Dash puts on his helmet, he will turn magical. It also has a pair of transparent wings to help it fly. Its power is releasing 100 000 volts of electricity.

2D Man
In Ch 6

Created & written by
Gavin Yi, 11
Assisted by Alia Kong, 10
Illustrated by Vicky Ding, 12

Freddie was a space explorer from SPYS Star. His job is to discover secrets of the universe and find new planets. He has black curly hair and wears a white technologically enhanced spacesuit with a '2D' label. The spacesuit is very light, which makes it easy for space explorers to move around. When he turns into the 2D man,He becomes as thin as paper. His spacesuit changes from white to orange and burgundy. His space helmet turns into a pair of Artificial Intelligence integrated shades.

He can turn 2D objects into reality and can wiggle through cracks, even microns. He can fold himself very small so he can be easily transported. He has a bottle to trap enemies and a sword that can turn things into a normal piece of paper. . Freddie can't touch water or else he will flop over and need a long time to bc dried off.

227

Freddie has a medium sized golden retriever named Longbottom. He is Freddie's best companion and travels with Freddie all over the galaxy. He is as thin as freddy and has the power of controlling poker cards. He can store things into the poker cards and reuse them again. He can create portals called Poker Doors with his poker cards, to transport Freddie and other superheroes to faraway places.

CG, Candy Girl
In Ch 9

Created & written by
Zenice Soo, 9
Assisted by Alia Kong, 10

Sunny is a new student at the Kids Power Academy. She is a princess from Candy Planet. . Sunny is a friendly and helpful girl. She always cheers up other students and helps the teacher carry their stuff around. She has big round eyes and long purple hair. She always munches on a lollipop and carries a bag of all-flavored bonbons. Her favorite outfit is a magenta hoodie with sparkly silver sneakers. Sunny is still in training to be a chemist at SPYS Stars.

When Sunny transforms into Candy Girl, she will tie her hair into long wavy pigtails and wear a ruby tiara on her head along with a purple mask. She will dress in a hoodie dress and strap it with a belt. She put on a pair of purple gloves and a pair of tall lace up booties.

Candy Girl can turn different kinds of candies into different powers. The candies can be used for granting new powers to the heroes. And due to all the candies Candy Girl has been eating, the corn syrup from the lollipops hardens in her mouth, so she can shoot out sugar bullets! When she fights, she has a candy stick, like a lollipop, to whack enemies. . It is super sticky and it turns the enemies into crying babies. The stick could also be used for hypnosis due to its spiral pattern.

Cupcake is an Alicorn from Planet Rainbow. She has a rainbow mane and a golden horn. She also has a pair of soulful eyes and white pearly wings. Cupcake's powers are producing healing cupcakes with her horn to heal scarred people. And she can shoot cupcake bombs at enemies.

Dr. David In Ch 9

Created & written by
Derek Ma, 10
Assisted by Alia Kong, 10

Derek is a chemist, he loves to do experiments on chemical substances. Derek spends a lot of time looking at the mirror grooming himself. He needs to go out in his best look every day. He is a germaphobe. He doesn't like to touch anything with his bare hands, so he always wears gloves. His daily outfit is a fine black tuxedo with brown leather shoes. He also wears a pair of black glasses.

When he transforms into David, he wears a brown fedora and a pair of blue smart glasses. His hair turns purple. He dressed in a technologically enhanced gray suit with a belt carrying needle bullets.

His primary power is Telekinesis. He can move things with his mind without touching them. He can control the object in any state of matter. He can also extract chemical compounds from any objects and mix them into explosive substances. They fuel the needle bullets as an atomic bomb.

231

His fedora acts like a vacuum. It can suck anything within 10 km, there is no size limit. The fedora can grow big to trap villains inside.

He has a black scorpion named Hottentotta. He can turn into a red scorpion. He is 23cm and always rests on David's shoulder when they are in battle. Hottentota can produce fatal colored venom and blast it out from his barb to attack enemies. Hottentotta may look fierce, but he is scared of any kind of wiggly worms and slithering snakes.

The Crossing Girl
In Ch 10

Created & written by
Joia Zhao, 11
Main Contributor to Ch 10

July is 11 years old. She is from Earth. She is a kind and courageous girl and always helps people in need. She is fond of animals. She loves to solve Mathematical problems. She wants to be an astronaut and protect the universe. She also loves making new friends. Her best friend is Spring. July has big blue eyes and a small mouth. She ties her long, curly hair into pigtails every day. Her favorite outfit is a blue T-shirt and jeans with a pair of trainers.

When July transforms into Crossing girl, she writes C-R-O-S-S-I-N-G in the air with her finger and says "Crossing Girl'. Her hair will turn blue and purple, and a pair of smart glasses and a headset will appear on her face. They were used to communicate with other superheroes. She will also put on a pair of rollerblades to glide across oceans or rivers to reach any location.

Crossing Girl's power is Time Travelling. She can travel back in time or fast forward in time to see past and future events. She can also summon portals called Crossing Holes by typing the location she wants to go to on her Typing Box, and use her Crossing Torch to make a Crossing Hole. Only Crossing Girl can use these gadgets. Other people who touch them will be struck by lightning. Crossing Girl is afraid of fire. She always needs TC to calm her down when she's near flames.

TC is Crossing Girls companion. TC is a cloud from Planet Sky. It is soft, can change in size. It has eyes and mouth. It can see, hear and talk. It carries Crossing Girl everywhere in the sky. It protects Crossing Girl from falling or coming into impact. Crossing Girl is the only one who can see TC's existence.

When the Kids Power Society asked me to help with their second book, I knew I had to say yes. These kids have something valuable to offer an adult writer such as myself. They still know how to have fun! Working with them, reminded me how important it is to play.

Editor and writer Alia Kong, only 10 years old, wanted to create a main character similar to Monty from my book series *Montgomery Schnauzer P.I.* as a "guest star" in their stories. I liked her ideas, and with a little tweaking, Monty fit well in the Kids Power universe. He's a little different than in my books, but he retains the qualities that make him unique: He is a detective. He is smart. He is still a dog and prone to doing doggy things. I was happy to give their depiction my paw-print stamp of approval.

In the middle of the project, the work became difficult, as often happens with writing. I am proud of these young writers for how they persevered. They never lost the sense of fun that inspired their stories in the first place. Their enthusiasm shows in the finished product.

As a middle grade novel written by middle grade kids, it has all the elements that kids love. It's larger than life with over-the-top characters and fantastic locations. It's full of action. It's full of comedy. But it also has heart. As young as they are, these kids know and care about the problems in our world. They've done what storytellers have done since time immemorial. They've put pen to paper to highlight these issues and offer a moral message to us, the readers.

I am honoured they chose me to participate in this project with them. Monty and I give this book two paws up.

Have a schnauzerrific day!

Timothy Forner
Author of *Montgomery Schnauzer P.I.*

ISBN 9798422808199

Made in the USA
Middletown, DE
28 June 2022